The
Real

Z

⭐ American Girl®

The Real Z

by Jen Calonita

Scholastic Inc.

Published by Scholastic Inc., *Publishers since 1920.* SCHOLASTIC and associated logos are trademarks and/or registered trademarks of Scholastic Inc. The publisher does not have any control over and does not assume any responsibility for author or third-party websites or their content.

Book design by Suzanne Lagasa

Author photo by April Mersinger Photography

Cover photos ©: girl: Michael Frost for Scholastic; puppy: Eric Isselee/ Shutterstock, Inc.

Excerpt from *Tenney* by Kellen Hertz

Tenney cover illustrations by Juliana Kolesova

ISBN 978-1-338-13705-7

10 9 8 7 6 5 4 3 2 1   17 18 19 20 21

Printed in the U.S.A. 58 • First printing 2017

For Keiran Cook, a true American Girl
and an excellent first reader

Contents

Chapter 1: **The Z. Crew**   1

Chapter 2: **Brainstorm Rainstorm**   11

Chapter 3: **School Daze**   23

Chapter 4: **Coffee Talk**   35

Chapter 5: **Lights, Camera, Action!**   46

Chapter 6: **Showtime**   58

Chapter 7: **Total Pro**   69

Chapter 8: **Rainy Week Blues**   80

Chapter 9: **Sneak Peek**   95

Chapter 10: **What's Your Story?**   105

Chapter 11: **The Real Me**   114

Chapter 12: **"The Horrible Homework Hacker"**   125

Chapter 13: **My Big Night**   132

Chapter 14: **A Fresh Start**   143

Chapter 1
The Z. Crew

I took one last look through my camera viewfinder. This was it.

My favorite moment in every video I shot.

Two seconds before I pressed RECORD, my palms usually began to sweat, my heart beat out of my chest, and I got more excited than my dog, Popcorn, when she knew she was going for a walk.

With my eye still glued to the viewfinder, I asked, "Lauren, can you raise Kit's hand an inch?" Lauren McClain, a.k.a. my best friend, production partner, and all-around amazing prop designer, was sitting on my bedroom floor posing my Kit Kittredge doll in front of a prop mountain as we worked on a video about the California gold rush for social studies. She moved Kit's tiny hand carefully and I zoomed in on it.

"Now can you turn the pencil she's holding so it really looks like she's writing on the pad?" Lauren adjusted the pad and pencil, which she had made out of sticky notes and a straw. I squinted harder as I stared through the camera lens and looked at the shot of Kit again. "Perfect! We're ready."

I pulled my purple knit beanie down on my head—I couldn't press RECORD without my good luck charm—and got ready to say my favorite word.

"Action!" I shouted. I snapped a photo of Kit. "And cut!"

I turned to my two computer screens—one was a larger monitor that I used to view all the stop-motion shots I had taken—and the second was my laptop with my webcam recording the whole shoot. I wanted to post the video for a new segment I'd been trying called "On Set with Me, Z!" The videos were a how-to guide to doing stop-motion videos like the kind I made. (Which meant I was shooting a video *inside* a video—how cool is that?) "Okay, Z. Crew, so maybe that wasn't the *most* exciting two seconds of filming in the world, but guess what? Every shot in our stop-motion videos is important," I said to my webcam.

"Especially when we get a close-up of those award-worthy props," Lauren chimed in, off camera.

Lauren is not a huge fan of being filmed, but she

loves working on AGSM (American Girl stop-motion) videos with me. We got the idea to do an AGSM video for our social studies assignment—a class presentation about a pivotal point in history—during lunch. Making videos is what we did for fun, which meant now we could have fun doing our homework.

I adjusted the webcam to focus on Lauren's prop work. "Look at this, Z. Crew. Lauren made a papier-mâché mountain out of some recycled newspaper she painted brown with flecks of gold. She is a total genius!" Lauren grinned. "She's going to win an Oscar for set design one day, right, Popcorn?" I asked my dog.

Popcorn barked and wagged her tail happily and jumped up on my legs. She was always jumping, like popcorn when it pops, which just happened to be my favorite snack in the world. It was also how my dalmatian got her name.

My Kit doll was standing on the fabric background that was our set—dark green, to represent trees in the distance—and a box light drenched the scene in warm, bright light. My room looked like a mini movie studio. The special equipment was all I wanted for my thirteenth birthday, and I've used it a ton since then.

I turned back to my camera, focused on the scene,

and Lauren raised Kit's hand as if she was waving. I snapped a shot. Then she raised it again a bit higher. "Each time we move Kit, we take another picture," I explained. "When we edit all the shots together, it will look like Kit is moving. But if we move Kit too quickly, the stop-motion will look really jerky. We want the scene to look seamless."

"Show them how we map out our stories," Lauren said, sounding excited. She was getting as into our vlogs as I was.

I pointed my webcam at a dry-erase board in the open cabinet attached to my desk. "Stop-motion videos need twelve pictures per second. So for a one-minute video, that's more than seven hundred shots! It's easy to get off track or forget something. That's why I map it all out first."

I zoomed in on a second whiteboard, which had lots of words written in different colors and pictures I'd cut out from magazines.

"This is my Brainstorm Board," I explained. "It's where the magic happens. You never know when inspiration will strike! Once I have my ideas and my storyboard, I put together a list of all the steps I have to take—like making props, sets, costumes, and editing—to create an awesome video. Just remember: A good director is nothing without her crew. Sometimes they look at things in a way you didn't even think of."

I reached over and grabbed a piece of caramel popcorn from the bowl Lauren was holding. "Like this," I said. "Lauren had the idea to use caramel popcorn for 'gold.'" I popped the piece in my mouth.

"After we're finished with our last few shots today, we'll layer in Kit's narration on how the gold rush led to the creation of the state of California."

"The movie is only five minutes long, but we've been working on it for three weeks," Lauren said.

"Making videos takes time," I told our viewers, "but it's worth it when the video turns out awesome!"

I caught a glimpse of myself on the monitor and suddenly had one of those "I can't believe I'm doing this" moments. A year ago, I never imagined I'd be a vlogger. Or that I'd have thousands of subscribers watching my AGSM videos or my "On Set with Me, Z!" videos. It all started one day when my friend Mariela was over. We were watching a video of a cat doing somersaults and a WATCH NEXT link popped up. I clicked on it and it was a stop-motion film featuring American Girl dolls. Lauren, Mari, and I had been making up stories with our American Girl dolls for years, but we'd never thought about filming them before. I showed my mom, who is a filmmaker herself, and she agreed I should try it.

That night I made my first stop-motion video. It was called "Samantha and the Saga of the Dropped Ice Cream Cone." After that, I was hooked. Now my American Girl stop-motion videos have hundreds of thousands of views, and Mom says not a day goes by without me filming something—even if it's just our mail carrier making a delivery!

Crunch, crunch, crunch.

What was that sound?

Lauren and I turned around. Popcorn's head was buried in our gold. She'd eaten every last kernel! She looked up and wagged her tail. Lauren and I burst out laughing.

"Oh, Popcorn!" I scratched her behind her ears. "You're calling break time, huh?" I turned my webcam back toward myself. "I guess that's a wrap. Z. Crew out!"

After dinner, I would do a quick edit of the vlog footage from the shoot and then show it to Mom and Dad. They viewed all my vlogs before I posted them. "Once you put something online for everyone to see, you can never take it back," Dad was always reminding me.

I helped Lauren pick up the props and put them safely in my closet so Popcorn couldn't trample (or eat!) them again. Kit got a place of honor on my bookshelf with the other dolls who'd already had their star turns in my AGSM videos.

Ping!

A new e-mail notification popped up on my computer. I slid into my purple desk chair and clicked on the e-mail. "No. Way," I said aloud.

It was from the CloudSong Seattle Film Festival. The festival had a young filmmaker contest that I'd entered on a whim last month just to see if I could get in. I could feel my heart race. "Lauren, pinch me!"

"What's wrong?" Lauren's voice was panicked. "Did today's video not save?"

That was always her biggest fear. It was one of my mine, too, second only to a movie critic someday giving one of my films only one star.

"The video is fine, but read this e-mail and tell me if I'm dreaming!" I couldn't believe what I was seeing.

Lauren leaned over my shoulder. "We are pleased to accept Suzanne Yang into the CloudSong Seattle Film Festival Young Filmmakers' Contest to create a short documentary film for this year's festival!" she read, using my real name, Suzanne. Everyone calls me Z, but I use my full name for report cards or contests that require your legal name—like this one!

"Z! This is HUGE!" Lauren clapped my shoulder. "It says they want you to create a ten-minute film about your life in Seattle and the top two films will be shown at the festival." She kept reading and then poked me. "First prize is fifteen hundred dollars!"

"I can't believe I got in." I felt dazed. "I get to make a real movie."

Lauren gave me a look. "You already make real movies." She motioned toward my camera and Brainstorm Board. "You're a great filmmaker."

I grinned. *"We're* great filmmakers," I said, because, after all, we were a team. "But this is legit!" I quickly read more of the e-mail. "It even says the CloudSong Festival gives you a grant: three hundred dollars to rent film equipment for my video or to get permits for shooting around Seattle."

Lauren's eyes widened. "How long do you have?"

"Six weeks." It wasn't much time, but I could already see the movie coming together in my head. I knew I could do this, even if a teensy part of me was panicked because I'd never been part of anything this big before.

"I bet you can do it in five," Lauren said confidently.

Lauren was not only my best friend: She was my own personal cheerleader. And her whole soccer team's. She was our middle school's star player, but she also always made sure everyone she played with knew they were MVPs, too.

"I guess I should go downstairs. My dad will be here any minute. I still have math homework to do, and I am not looking forward to two pages of multiplying fractions." Lauren's mouth curled into a deep frown. I knew how hard she worked for her good grades.

"Want to work on our math homework together?" I asked.

"It's okay. I'll wait till I get home." Lauren hefted her backpack. Her favorite soccer ball, a neon-green-and-black one, hung from the mesh sack on the front. She grinned suddenly. "Want to send a quick video message to Mari, Gigi, and Becka to tell them your big news?"

"Let's do it!" I answered, grabbing my cell phone. The two of us sat down on my bed. Popcorn bounded up behind us and stuck her nose between our shoulders. The three of us just fit into the small frame. I hit RECORD, and then we made a series of funny faces and poses (well, Popcorn didn't). "Lauren and I are celebrating! I have something major to tell you guys when we chat tomorrow!" Then I sent the video to our group chat.

This was my big break. I could feel it. And I couldn't wait to share the news with my friends.

Chapter 2

Brainstorm
Rainstorm

Dad had made kimchi stew for dinner (a Korean dish his grandmother had taught him to make with pork, scallions, vegetables, and tofu). As we settled in around the table, Mom shared the highlights from her day. She had worn her long black hair down, and I could see her work lanyard still around her neck. My mom teaches film, but also makes her own movies. She's usually the first person I bounce ideas off of. I may have inherited my dad's sometimes quirky sense of humor, but I got my love of filmmaking from my mom.

Sharing the highs and the lows from our day was our nightly family tradition, but Mom had jumped in before I could break the exciting news about CloudSong. I had so much to tell them! Without realizing it, I started tapping my spoon against my bowl as Mom talked about the university film study class she was teaching.

"And one of the students had never seen the original *Star Wars* films, can you believe it?" she said. Then she noticed my excitement. "Z?" She glanced at the spoon that I was using like a drumstick. I immediately stopped. "What's wrong?"

"Sorry," I said. "My good news tonight is huge and if I don't tell you soon, I may explode."

"Well, we don't want that to happen," Dad said, looking at me over the top of his glasses. Mom nodded. "Tell us."

I took a deep breath. I could hear the *ticktock* of the cuckoo clock, which had been in my mother's family for more than a hundred years (and came all the way from Korea in my great-grandmother's suitcase!).

"I got accepted into the CloudSong Seattle Film Festival Young Filmmakers' Contest!" I said so quickly it almost sounded like one long word. Mom dropped her spoon. "They're giving me three hundred dollars to make a short film about Seattle!"

"That's incredible!" Dad cheered. Popcorn jumped

up and down next to the table and barked to be part of the conversation.

Mom reached her hand across the table. Her eyes were teary. "I am so proud of you! Our Z—a real filmmaker."

"Should I be nervous?" I asked. "I'm flipping out!" They laughed.

Mom nodded. I could already see her filmmaker mind at work. "Of course you are. This is a big deal!"

"Tell us more about the grant," Dad said, running a hand through his black hair. "What's your deadline? Do you need our help at all?"

Dad was so organized. Being an aerospace engineer, he had to be. He helped design airplanes for a living and was always working on a bunch of projects at the same time. I quickly filled them in on the contest rules and details.

Dad listened carefully, drumming his fingers on the table. "Seattle . . . hmm . . . that's a lot to cover in one documentary."

"I guess so," I said. I looked at Mom. "I'm still just so surprised that I even got this grant."

Mom grabbed a pen from the buffet table behind

us. "Dad's right. Movies need a clear story or they get messy. You'll have to decide what your vision is."

I nodded. "Well, I'm not sure if this counts as a *vision*, but I guess I would want everyone to see Seattle like I do—as the greatest city in the world."

"Now you're talking!" said Dad. "What makes it so great?"

I thought for a moment. "I like that I can walk Popcorn down the block or go paddleboarding on Lake Union."

Mom wrote the idea down on her napkin.

Now that it was spring, we'd be able to take our two-seater sea kayak back out. Which also meant . . . "And flying kites on Kite Hill." Mom wrote that down, too.

"Don't forget Mount Rainier National Park," Dad added. "We hike there at least once a month."

"And Seward Park is great for bike riding. Lauren and I love when you take us there."

Mom handed Dad the pen, and he wrote both ideas down. Ten minutes later, both sides of the napkin were full. The list had grown to our top fifteen places that made Seattle home. And I was only getting started! I couldn't wait to run upstairs and start writing things down on my Brainstorm Board.

"You're excused," Mom said, the second I finished my last bite of stew and gave her a pleading look.

"Thank you!"

I ran upstairs with Popcorn on my heels and hopped onto the computer to research which landmarks required permits for filming. I'd barely started when my phone pinged with group text messages from my friends.

> **MARIELA:** Z!! What's the big news?
> **GIGI:** Lauren?! Can you tell us?
> **LAUREN:** It's your news, Z, not mine!
> **BECKA:** Tell us! Tell us! Tell us!

I started to laugh. I quickly typed back.

> **Z:** Okay, I'll tell you guys. Drumroll, please . . .
> **MARIELA:** WAIT. I'm coming over! I want to hear this in person!
> **GIGI:** Hurry, Mari!

While I waited for Mari to arrive from the house next door, I wrote down some notes. *Gum Wall closeup—gross or cool? Include the Beanery! Must show everyone Queen Anne Hill.* That was my neighborhood. It sat on the highest peak in the city, northwest of downtown Seattle. I loved eating at outdoor restaurants with my parents and going biking with Mariela. Ooh! Maybe I could wear my GoPro camera and film Seattle by bike, too! I jotted that idea down as well. I heard a knock at my door, and Popcorn started barking, wagging her tail madly to welcome our visitor.

"Come in!" I yelled, spinning around in my chair.

"Whatisitwhatisitwhatisit," Mariela said quickly as she bent down to pet Popcorn then rushed over to my desk. Her cheeks were flushed like she'd been jogging, but she looked ready for the runway in a slouchy white scarf that she'd paired with a cute, fringed navy shirt and bright green skinny jeans. I'd never think to put those items together, but they looked great on Mari, especially the white scarf against her bronze skin and curly black hair. She plopped down on my bed, and a stack of beaded bracelets on her arm slid down to her wrist, sounding like a wind chime. "You can't tease me like this! What's your big news?"

Mari is my oldest friend in the world. She's the one who started calling me Z when I was a toddler and it stuck. She's one year older *and* in a cool band, but she still finds time to play official fashion consultant for

Lauren and me on our AGSM videos. (Kit had Mari to thank for her rocking knit hat and sweater with jeans in our California gold rush video.)

"Hmm . . ." I scratched my head. "I don't know if I'm ready to spill the beans yet." Mari's jaw dropped and I laughed. "I'm just kidding! Get over here so that we can chat with Becka and Gigi." I waved her to my desk.

I quickly set up a video chat, and soon saw little moving images of my friends staring back at me from the computer screen.

"Finally!" Gigi said in a gorgeous British accent that made even the most mundane words ("bottle," "water," "class") sound *so* much better. Her red hair was pulled into a high ponytail, and she had on flannel pj's. (She's from London, but her dad is a diplomat and she had mentioned earlier in the week that they were visiting DC. It was almost bedtime there.)

"We can't stand the suspense anymore!" Becka urged. "Look what you're making me do: Pop-a-wheelies!" She spun her wheelchair in front of the screen, her blonde hair whipping around her face. Mari, Gigi, and I all applauded. "Now I'm dizzy! What's going on?"

I looked at my friends' eager faces. I had known

Mari forever, but Becka, Gigi, and I had only met last year at VidCon (one of the largest video conferences in the world) in Southern California. We like to say it was fate that our parents all took us and we happened to be in line behind one another to meet one of our favorite vloggers. We spent two hours nonstop chatting, and by the time we made it to the front of the line, we were already BFFs!

We exchanged numbers, and soon Becka and I were sending each other silly videos (like the one I did of Popcorn and me ballroom dancing and one Becka made of herself doing the coolest basketball twirling hand trick I'd ever seen). Gigi goes with her dad a lot when he travels for work, and she liked to vlog about the cool foods she tried in different countries. When she did a post from South Korea about not liking Pocky sticks, I told her she had to try the chocolate-covered desserts again because they were the best thing ever! We were constantly sending each other snack packs. (Recently, I'd sent Gigi Crab Chips and she'd sent me hard-to-find Cadbury chocolate you can only get in the United Kingdom.)

"Okay, ready?" I asked.

"YES," my friends shouted.

"I got accepted to the CloudSong Film Festival. They want me to do a documentary about Seattle!" I shouted.

All three of them squealed and yelled "congratulations!" and "well done!" (that was Gigi). Popcorn barked and chased her tail. I gave them all the details, including how I was being given three hundred dollars to help cover any expenses for the film.

"There is this special camera mount that I've been dying to test out—you should definitely try to rent one!" Becka said. "It has six cameras going at once so you can basically get a panoramic shot. You'd be able to shoot some great views of Seattle like that."

"That *is* cool," I agreed, writing down the words "panoramic camera mount." "Maybe I can get a shot of the Seattle shipyards and the Locks using that."

"You could open on that shot," Mari suggested.

"Yeah, maybe," I said. Dad and I liked watching the salmon swim upstream at the Locks, but we didn't do it that often. Still, it was definitely famous.

"Maybe you should rent a drone so you can fly a camera over the city and get amazing aerial shots of your favorite landmarks," Gigi suggested.

"Oh yes! That would be great for the Space Needle," Mari said.

"Yeah, that's a good idea," I agreed, and added "aerial shots" to my list. The judges would definitely want to see the Space Needle in a movie about Seattle, right?

"Next question: What are you going to wear if you appear on camera?" Mari asked. "Because I already have some thoughts. You look great in greens. I can even lend you green rain boots if you're shooting in the rain." Her eyes lit up. "And you could do a segment on Seattle fashion. You love Beat Street Thrift Store."

"I got my directing hat there," I said, and grabbed my purple beanie off my desk. I placed it on my head. "Maybe I could interview you there!"

"I can be in your movie?" Mari asked.

"Of course!" I said.

Fashion, friends, aerial views of Seattle, and panoramic shots of the city. Plus, stops at all the landmarks I talked about with Mom and Dad. Wow, there was a lot to squeeze into a ten-minute movie! I remembered what Mom said about movies needing a vision, but I wasn't sure I had one yet. I had a lot of pieces so far, but no idea how they all fit together. I had a lot of work to do.

"Thanks, guys," I told my friends. "You've given me awesome new ideas."

"I'll send you links to some of that camera equipment," Becka said.

"And I'll send you this great video about planning your shots. The girl who posted it made everything in her vlog look cool and artsy," Gigi said, yawning. "Sorry! Definitely have to go to sleep soon."

"I'll bring over wardrobe choices," Mari added.

They were all being so helpful, but I felt my brain beginning to fog up—it was a lot to process. "Perfect." I looked at my list. It was twice as long as it was before.

"Ring if you need help," said Gigi. "We're headed to Buenos Aires this week, but you know how to find me." We all oohed. Gigi went to the coolest places.

After we all said our good-byes, and Becka and Gigi's video screens went dark, it was just Mari and me. I pulled my purple beanie cap down on my head and stared at my Brainstorm Board, my thoughts swirling. I was in director mode! *Vision.* I needed to make sense of all these notes and find my vision.

"Oh! Another lightbulb," Mari said. "Maybe you should film my band playing at the Beanery on Tuesday. I mean, if you want."

I didn't really need any more ideas for my documentary, but listening to Mari's band was one of my favorite things to do. "That would be really cool. Besides, I already have my fan tee made." I ran over to my closet and pulled out the purple shirt I'd been working on. I'd torn the sleeves off, added black bubble-paint lettering that said *Needles in a Haystack*, and drew a simple picture of the Seattle Space Needle (the inspiration for the band's name).

Mari came over and thumbed the dried bubble paint. "This shirt is ah-mazing! Z, you might have a side career in the music tee business."

"I'm a little busy for that," I joked, pulling on my hat again. "I've got a movie to make first." I sighed and turned back to the Brainstorm Board, jumping back into Z Director Mode.

"Z, don't worry," Mari said as she patted me on the back. "Your movie is going to be great—especially if *I'm* in it." We both laughed. Mari was right, worrying wasn't going to get me anywhere. There was no time to waste.

Chapter 3

School Daze

*O*pen *with a fade-in of my house, then cut to me sitting on my front steps. I'll introduce viewers to Seattle starting small—my house, my block, my neighborhood. Hmm . . . Is that flashy enough? Maybe I should start with the Locks or the Space Needle instead, like Mari suggested? But where would I go from there? Hmm . . . What if I . . .*

"Z?"

Oh, I could maybe do one of those 360-degree views of my street if I rent that . . .

"Z? Do you have the answer?"

I looked up, startled.

Ms. Garner was standing in front of the SMART Board with her pointer tapping at a multiplication fraction equation. My math teacher's eyes were only on me. I could hear my classmates trying to hold in their laughter. I glanced at Lauren, who was sitting in the row across from me. She bit her lip.

I quickly snapped to attention. "Yep!" I said, and tried to stall for time. "I just need one more second to figure this out." I scrawled some numbers on my notebook as I tried to think of the answer. I peeked at the board again. Whew! Thankfully this question wasn't too hard and I knew the answer. "If you simplify three-sixths and make it one-third and multiply it by two-thirds, the answer would be . . . two-ninths."

Mrs. Garner gave me a meaningful look. "That is correct, Z. Thank you for contributing to the class discussion."

"You're welcome," I said, feeling my cheeks start to burn. *That was close!* I didn't take my eyes off the board for the remainder of class. When it was time to leave and head to our free period, Lauren was waiting for me in the hall.

"You are so lucky you're good at math," she said once we were out of earshot of Ms. Garner's room. We headed down the crowded hallway, dodging and weaving past groups of students. "I would have been toast."

"No, I was just lucky it was an easy question," I said as we turned down a new hall and headed toward the media room. It was off the library and had banks of computers that students could use for projects. It was also where Camera Club met twice a week during free period with Mr. Mullolly, our faculty advisor. Each week, we made a news segment about school happenings that was shown on the SMART Boards in the classrooms on Friday afternoons.

"Oh, by the way," Lauren told me as we neared the media room, "I got really inspired after soccer practice last night and wrote a script for a new AGSM video! I'm calling it 'The Horrible Homework Hacker.'" Lauren whipped some pages out of a binder and handed them to me. "Be honest and tell me if it's any good."

"I'm sure it's great," I said, sticking the pages in my shiny silver-and-green polka-dot folder. It was where I kept my ideas for Camera Club. "I love the title!"

"Good." Lauren grinned. "I'm so excited about the story! We should get together one day this week and finish up our Kit gold rush video so you can concentrate on the CloudSong project."

"I've got the Kit stuff under control," I told her. "There are just voice-overs and sound to add in."

"I want to help you," Lauren insisted. "It's a group project. You shouldn't have to do it alone."

"Hi, girls," Mr. Mullolly interrupted as the bell for

class rang. He rushed past us. "Coming to the meeting?"

I smiled. Mr. Mullolly was one of my favorite teachers. He drew funny pictures on the SMART Board every day, and shared my love of old movies. "Wouldn't miss it," I said, rushing in the door behind him. I scanned the crowded room for seats and saw two people waving to us. Andrew and Maddie had saved us seats. The four of us had met last fall when we all joined Camera Club.

"We thought you got lost," Andrew said as I slid into a chair across from Maddie, who was reading the sports section of the school newspaper. She passed it over to me and pointed to a picture of Lauren scoring the winning goal at last Saturday's game.

"Nice one, Lauren," Maddie said, her brown eyes bright. "You're putting this school on the Seattle map."

"So are you, Miss No-Hitter," Lauren said, and Maddie's cheeks reddened. She covered her face with her curly brown hair, but Andrew nudged her shoulder.

"Don't be embarrassed!" he told her. "You won us the game!"

Andrew and Maddie were on the baseball team. Maddie was their ace pitcher and the only girl in the league!

Maddie always fought Lauren over who got to cover sports, and Andrew and I battled it out over who got the juiciest news assignment of the week, but it was friendly competition.

"Okay, before we get started, I want to share the great response we got to last week's show," Mr. Mullolly said, and the room settled down. "Everyone is still talking about the interview some of you did with Quackers the football mascot last week. Everybody got a kick out of Andrew's quacking translations." Andrew stood up and bowed. We all cheered. "Maybe we should consider a follow-up story since people keep stopping me in the halls asking who the real Quackers is. Any takers?" Maddie's hand shot up. "Okay, Maddie, it's yours." Mr. Mullolly went through a few more segments we had done and talked about some upcoming school events we needed to cover. Lauren and I volunteered to cover the soccer team's first night game against Riverside in a few weeks. Lauren would do the "team bench" report during the game and I would film fan reactions.

"And now the bad news," Mr. Mullolly said, and held up the camera we all took turns using for filming. "Our camera broke this past weekend when it was accidentally tripped over at the football game." Everyone groaned. "I know, bad luck. Worse, the repair costs are so high that it might not even be worth saving."

Maddie spoke up. "But it's the only camera we have. How are we supposed to film our segments?"

Everyone mumbled in agreement. I felt my heart drop. This was my favorite school activity. I really hoped the club wouldn't be canceled till we could buy a new camera.

"I spoke to the principal and there's not enough money left in the budget this spring to replace the camera," Mr. Mullolly said. "And I know we have already agreed we need more than one camera for a group this big anyway. In the meantime, we're just going to have to improvise." He smiled. "You guys are reporters. I know you can think on your feet." Some of the kids looked skeptical.

"This stinks," Andrew said, leaning in so only Lauren, Maddie, and I could hear. "People are finally talking about our videos and now we can't even make one."

"Maybe we can use our phones," I suggested.

"That doesn't look professional," he grumbled, pushing his light brown hair out of his eyes. "Everyone films on their phones."

"Andrew has a point," I said.

Maddie rolled her eyes. "Don't encourage him, Z! He's being a downer." Andrew poked her shoulder, and she poked him back. "It's true!"

"What can we do?" I said. "It's not like we can come up with the kind of money to buy a new camera."

"Maybe we could win the money," Andrew said. "Everyone tell their parents to play the lottery."

Maddie and Lauren laughed, but I froze. *Win the money.* Maybe I could do that!

"Hold on a second. Andrew isn't crazy," I said. "Maybe we *could* win the money." My friends looked at me. "I just got accepted to a film festival, and if my film is the top entry, I win fifteen hundred dollars."

"Whoa!" Andrew leaned back in his chair. "That's enough for Mariners season tickets!"

"Or new video equipment," Lauren said. "Z, you'd really do that if you won?"

"Why not?" I said with a shrug. "I already have my own equipment at home, and this way I'd still get to use the new camera to film Maddie and Andrew decorating the gym for Spring Bash or Lauren winning a soccer game."

"Those things are all going to happen, so you better win that contest fast," Andrew teased. "Seriously, Z, it would be so cool if you did that."

I felt good inside. Maybe CloudSong would turn out to be more than just my chance to prove I was a real filmmaker. Maybe it would be my chance to help my club, too.

Still pumped up from our conversation in the Camera Club meeting, I decided to shoot a rainy day scene with Popcorn as soon as I got home from school. Mom and I had watched a video Gigi had sent of a girl filming herself on a walk that made you feel like you were actually in the girl's shoes. It looked really cool. I wrangled Popcorn into her raingear so I could give it a try. Once we were outside, I got out my camera and began to record. It wasn't raining at the moment, but there were plenty of puddles, and everything was wet from the day's showers.

"Popcorn takes a walk, take one," I said as I held the camera out in front of me and started walking down the quiet street.

I zoomed in tight on Popcorn's raincoat and adorable hat and filmed a shot of her sniffing the grass. Then I slowly zoomed out so that the viewer could see our whole street, from the different style houses to the gardens and hilly lawns. As Popcorn trotted along happily, I held the camera steady.

Then Popcorn spotted her archenemy: the squirrel.

Popcorn began barking like crazy and tugged on the leash. I tried to hold on tight as the squirrel went up the nearest tree and Popcorn attempted to follow. I tried pulling Popcorn away—even though this was a pretty sweet action scene. Then the squirrel jumped and took off down the sidewalk. Popcorn darted after her, and I struggled to hang on to my camera. In the process, I felt Popcorn's leash slip out of my hand.

"Popcorn, wait!" I panicked, running down the sidewalk after her as she took off at a full sprint. The squirrel dove left into the street, and Popcorn tore off after her, just as a car came cruising by.

"Popcorn!" I screamed. The car screeched to a stop, and Popcorn kept going to the other side of the street where the squirrel went up the tree and disappeared. Popcorn sat down, wagging her tail, and looked over at me as if to say, *What?* My heart was pounding out of my chest as I held up my hand to the car to thank the driver for stopping, looked both ways, and dashed across the street after my dog. When I reached her, I pulled her in tight.

"Don't . . . ever . . . do . . . that . . . again," I told Popcorn. Popcorn just wagged her tail.

"Z!" Mom cried, running down the block. "I just pulled in and heard a squeal of tires." She leaned down to me and Popcorn, placing a hand on both of us. I could see worry written all over her face. "What happened?"

"I was trying to shoot a scene with Popcorn, but she spotted a squirrel and I was trying to hold on to my camera and she got away from me. I couldn't keep hold of her leash." My eyes welled with tears, and Popcorn tried to lick my face.

"She's okay," Mom said, pulling me in for a hug. "And you are, too, thank goodness, but you can't be careless, Z. You're trying to do too much at once. You could have waited and asked me for help."

"You're right," I admitted, wiping my eyes with the back of my sleeve. "I shouldn't have tried to do everything alone." I felt a drop fall on my head and looked up. It was starting to rain again.

"Come on," Mom said. "Let's get home before it starts to pour." We both held on to Popcorn's leash for safekeeping. My heart was still beating fast. I kept seeing Popcorn darting in front of that car.

Mom started humming to herself.

"What song is that?" I asked.

"Oh!" Mom looked embarrassed. "It's 'Singin' in the Rain.'" I looked at her blankly. "You know, from that movie with Gene Kelly." I shook my head. "It's a classic! I show it to my students every term." Mom started singing the song this time and I paid attention to the words.

> *I'm singing in the rain, just singin' in the rain*
> *What a glorious feeling, I'm happy again.*

And that's when I got it—a flash of genius, as my mom would call it.

Seattle was definitely not the rainiest city in the country, but it was famous for its drizzle. Having rain in my Seattle movie would be classic, just like this song, and I knew just who I could get to sing it. I'd ask Mariela's band, Needles in a Haystack, to do a remix of the song.

I could even shoot them playing the song . . . IN THE RAIN!

"Mom, you've saved the day," I said, putting an arm around her.

"I usually do," Mom said drily. "But remind me: Why am I being called Super Mom this time around?"

I held Popcorn's leash tighter and practically skipped down the sidewalk. "You just helped me figure out my movie's story, and it's going to be fantastic!"

Chapter 4

Coffee Talk

After school the next day, Lauren and I rode our scooters down the block from school to the Beanery, Mari's parents' coffee shop, to watch Mari's band play. I sang "Singin' in the Rain" the whole ride over. Mom had showed me the famous movie clip and I had to admit, it was the perfect song-and-dance scene. No wonder film students still studied it.

"Could you stop begging Mother Nature to make it rain?" Lauren joked as we pulled up to the bike rack and locked our scooters to it. "It's finally nice out and you want it to rain some more!"

"Hey, rain!" I shouted to the sun above. "I'm ready to sing in the rain! And dance around lamp-posts! Bring it on!" Lauren looked at me like I'd lost my mind. I cheered and spun around like I was Gene Kelly.

"I think you're dehydrated," she said as we headed inside the shop and heard the espresso machine whirring. Mari's mom was helping kids in line order bubble teas. People seated all around the shop at long wooden tables were talking to friends or working on their laptops. I spotted Mari's band setting up in the back corner, and Lauren and I went right over.

"Hey!" Mari said as she adjusted her mic stand. She was wearing a funky black shirt dress with a purple cinched belt. "I saved you two seats up front."

"You hold our spots while I order our drinks," Lauren told me. "Your usual?"

I put my fingers to my lips and pretended to think for a moment. "I'm feeling adventurous today. How about a strawberry and mango bubble tea with strawberry hearts instead?" I handed Lauren money from my pocket to pay.

"Perfect choice! I think I'll do the same. Be right back," she said, and headed up to the counter.

"Adventurous, huh?" Mari asked as her bandmates tuned up. "Is that why I saw Popcorn wearing your GoPro camera this morning on her walk before school?"

I groaned with embarrassment. "Yeah, I watched the winning film from CloudSong's Young Filmmakers'

Contest last year and was trying out something new. The filmmaker strapped his camera to a STOP sign and filmed people walking by, so I thought it might be cool to get a dog's view of town." I made a face. "Turns out that view is all grass and tree stumps." Mari laughed. "But that's okay because I have an even better idea for this doc. It involves you."

Mari's eyes widened. "Me?"

"Actually, your whole band," I said. "I was thinking about how Seattle's so rainy, and how it might be cool to include 'Singin' in the Rain'—what do you think of Needles in a Haystack doing a new version of that song?"

"Oh, I love that movie!" Mari said, and sang the song's chorus.

"The song is perfect," I said shyly. "But you know what would make it sound even better? If Needles in a Haystack put their own spin on it." Mari looked at me. "And then I could film it as a music video for my movie."

"What?" Mari screeched, and her bandmates all stopped what they were doing to look at us. "Are you serious?" I nodded. "Guys," Mari called to her friends. "Z wants to put us in her movie!" She quickly told them about the contest. They all huddled together talking while I stood anxiously outside their circle watching. Mari turned around and looked at me. "Okay, we're in! We'd love to be your rock stars!"

"Awesomesauce!" I cheered. I would have done a cartwheel if there was room, but there wasn't. Instead, I jumped up onstage and hugged every member of the band. "I'll let you guys get on with your show. Do you mind if I film you guys while you play today, though?" I asked Mari.

"Mind? We'd love it." Mari grinned. "Shoot away!"

I got out my camera, which I had put in my bag this morning, and started recording. I zoomed in on Lauren returning with our milky tea drinks. Tiny jelly strawberry hearts nestled at the bottom of the cups. I paused to take a sip of mine through the wide green straw and slurped up two strawberry hearts along with the sweet drink. Ahh . . . like liquid candy! I pressed RECORD as the band announced they were ready to go.

Needles in a Haystack called themselves a rock band, but I secretly thought they sounded pop, like some of my favorite songs on the radio. Either way, I loved their beat and their covers of popular songs. Lauren and I couldn't help but bop along. Lauren usually doesn't let me film her, but she even let me get a shot of her playing air drums. The whole Beanery was getting into the show!

Before their last song, Mari came up to the mic. "This is a new song, 'You Do You,' and it goes out to our favorite director, Z, who everyone is going to know soon!" Mari pointed to me in the audience. "This one is for you!"

Then Mari started to sing the song. The band totally killed it. I could practically see the music video I was going to make right in front of my eyes . . .

"Thank you, Beanery!" I heard Mari shout.

Mari jumped off the stage and plopped down next to me, beaming. "What did you think?"

"I think we are going to make the *best* music video," I said, and the two of us squealed. This movie was going to be unstoppable!

Now I just had to plan the music video shoot, and I knew just the place to do that: my favorite working spot, the film archive center at my mom's university. When Dad dropped me off there after school on Wednesday, I rushed into the building and soaked in the scent of film.

The *Real* Z

The film archive center just feels so magical. The shelves are filled with dusty, old film canisters and books on moviemaking, and there is a projector always whirring away in the background that screens a constant loop of silent film scenes on one wall. I found Mom bent over her laptop typing with a stack of books open in front of her.

"Hi, Mom," I whispered as I sat down across from her. The center was like a library so everyone was quiet in there. I always felt very professional sitting by my mom working on movie stuff.

"Hey, sweetie." Mom looked up with tired eyes as I pulled my laptop out of its case. She'd probably been poring over these books for hours. "What are you working on today?"

I told Lauren I was going to watch the Kit movie again to see if it needed any editing tweaks, but I was anxious to work on my CloudSong project. "I'm going to try to storyboard the music video I'm doing with Mari."

"Great idea," Mom said.

"But first, I'm going to see if anyone commented on my Z. Crew video post about CloudSong!"

"I could use a study break, too," Mom said as she scooted her chair over to my side of the table. Now that my family and friends knew about CloudSong, I wanted to see what the Z. Crew thought, too. I loaded the video and saw it already had several hundred likes. There were also a bunch of comments.

> **ABBYKICKS74:** Z!!! This. Is. Incredible. CONGRATS!
> **PERFECTLYPETRA872:** Love your videos, Z! Bet you win the whole thing!
> **AGMOVIELOVER12:** Good luck, Z! You won't need it, though. You got this!

Mom patted my back. "Look how happy everyone is for you," she said.

"I know." They were so supportive; it made me smile. I scrolled further down and my smile faded.

> **WHODOYOUVLOG89:** No one can beat Z! She is the master of AGSM!
> **NOTURAVGVLOGR:** True, but this isn't AGSM. It's a real movie. Z will have to make her film even better than usual.

NotURavgVlogR was right. I was making a short film, not a stop-motion video. I'd never done a documentary before. I had to make every shot in this film flawless if I wanted to win. It couldn't just be good. It had to be great.

"Z, you're not letting one comment mess with your head, are you?" Mom asked, seemingly reading my thoughts.

"No," I said quickly, and Mom raised an eyebrow at me. "Okay, maybe. But they're right." I pointed to the comment. "I always want people to think I know what I'm doing, but right now I feel like I really don't. If I want to have a shot at winning first place, I have to stand out. I can't have the judges think, 'This is pretty good *for a kid.*' I want them to say: 'Wow, we just found the next big thing.' My movie needs to be perfect."

Mom pushed her chair away from our table. "Come with me. I want to show you something." We crossed the archive, my rain boots squishing loudly as I walked on the carpet. Mom stopped for a moment to grab a film canister and then led me past the projection area, to the information desk where a student was standing behind the counter.

"Anything open, Gabe?" Mom asked. "I want to show my daughter something."

He smiled at my mom and me. "Sure, Professor Yang. The screening room is free. It's all yours."

I loved when the students called my mom Professor Yang. She was like a rock star here! I followed Mom down the hall and into a room. I exhaled slowly in awe. We were standing in a tiny, private movie theater! With a flick of a switch, the dusty velvet curtains parted to each side of a large screen. I sat down in one of the over-stuffed seats, and Mom quickly set up the film and lowered the lights.

At first, I wasn't sure what I was watching. It was just a series of short clips. Some of the clips were amazing, and some were pretty dull or jumpy like they were made by someone who didn't know how to use a camera. I looked over at Mom. She was watching the screen with interest.

"What is this?" I asked.

Mom smiled. "This is a clip reel from some of the first films famous filmmakers made—Nora Ephron, Steven Spielberg, J. J. Abrams, and Mira Nair—they're all in here. As you can see, they're not Oscar-worthy." A grainy shot of a crowd blurred in and out of focus. "But you know what's great about all of these scenes? Every one of these filmmakers gave it their best shot, and they learned something in the process. Every time you step behind the camera you learn something new."

I thought of my Popcorn cam. It hadn't worked, but it was fun to try.

"Remember I asked you the other night about your vision for your movie?" Mom asked. "That's your most crucial piece to the puzzle. You can't worry about what comments your Z. Crew posts or what your friends think you should film. What do *you* want your movie to say?"

I thought about it for a moment. "I want it to be like me, but bigger and better. I've started shooting, but I'm not sure any of the shots go together. Like I have walks around the neighborhood on my favorite street with Popcorn, and I shot Needles in a Haystack playing at the Beanery, but I don't have any of the big scenes I want to do yet, like the music video or any landmarks," I told Mom. "I still want to rent a drone camera to record all the boats moving through the channels at the waterfront."

"Wow, you've got a lot you want to do! You're taking chances," Mom said. I gave her a worried look—not sure if that was a good thing. "That's what directors do. Trying new things allows the filmmaking magic to happen." She put her arm around me and pulled me in tight.

Making filmmaking magic. I knew how to do that. I put my head on her shoulder. "Thanks, Professor Yang," I whispered.

"It's Mom to you," Mom teased. "And you're welcome."

We sat with our arms around each other and watched the movie until the projector went dark.

Chapter 5

Lights, Camera, Action!

MUSIC VIDEO SHOOT CHECKLIST:

1. Go over the day's schedule with the crew (a.k.a. Mom, Dad, and Lauren).

2. Double-, triple-, quadruple-check I have my camera AND that it works!

3. Equipment check: extension cords, tarps, and extra lights

4. Call the park again to make sure the reserved picnic area is absolutely, positively, definitely okay to shoot in. Bring the permit in case anyone asks to see it.

5. Go over Mari's costume picks with her one more time. Raincoats or no raincoats for the final shot?

6. Pick up food from deli! Don't forget snacks. Nothing greasy—it will ruin the costumes! (Mari's note, not mine.)

7. Pray the forecast for Saturday is right: 80% chance of rain.

I'd planned for a week and a half, and now it was finally time to shoot what could be the most important part of my movie—the Needles in a Haystack video—and the weather couldn't have been more perfect. The meteorologist was right! I could hear the *pat-pat-pat* of light rain hitting the gutter outside my bedroom window.

Rain was just what I needed to make the day's shoot a success. Well, that and about nine million other details that had to fall into place. I'd also looked at Mom's camera equipment to see what I could borrow, like extra tripods. I couldn't afford to rent them because I'd spent so much money renting a drone camera to use next week at the Locks. Dad had seemed skeptical about that decision. "I hope it's worth it, Z," he'd said. "You've always used your own camera, and your videos have turned out great." I didn't think Dad got it. I needed this movie to look *better* than my regular videos.

My bedroom was packed with video equipment, tagged props, backdrops, a rolling cart crammed with outfits (and second outfits) for every band member and colorful rain jackets and umbrellas we borrowed from everyone we knew. Mari still wasn't convinced we should have the girls use them. "Running in the rain without your jacket looks cooler," she had said. I looked at my watch. We'd figure it out. It was time to go. I grabbed my new director's clapboard from my dresser. The clapboard, which movie sets use to synchronize sound with the picture, was a gift from Mom and Dad. "Every director needs one!" Dad said. The clapboard looked like those old-fashioned black-and-white ones you saw in movies when someone stood in front of the camera and shouted, "Scene one, take one!" I'd always wanted one.

The next hour was a blur. Mom and I whizzed over to the community park by the house where we were shooting the video while Dad headed to the deli to get the food we'd ordered. The playground looked lonely. Since it was drizzling, no one was hanging out on the swings or climbing through the tubes. It was just us, which was perfect for shooting a video. We quickly set up our equipment and the pop-up tents we had to keep the cameras and Mari's band dry if it started raining really hard.

I looked up at the sky and let the rain hit my face. I had broken the shoot down in half-hour blocks of time. I knew the day's exact order of events. This was all really happening!

Two hours later, my confidence had snapped like a guitar string.

Literally. A guitar string broke and stopped the whole shoot.

"The guitarist can't play at all until her mom gets here with another string," Mari told me. "She didn't realize she didn't have extras with her."

"Can't she just pretend to play?" I made a mean air guitar motion. "No one will know, will they?" The actual song arrangement would be layered over the video during editing anyway.

Mari smiled sadly. "This is our first music video,

and she doesn't want to fake it." The rain started to fall harder as she spoke, and we huddled under my pink striped umbrella. "I'm sorry, Z."

"The wait could be a while," Dad said as he pulled his hood tighter around his head. "When I ran out for more tarps, there was a fallen tree in town, and they were redirecting traffic down side streets."

I glanced at the band hanging out under the large tarp with their equipment. I really wanted to record them playing their instruments in the rain, but it was much harder to shoot in bad weather than I realized. If it was drizzling, they could play for a bit, but if it started to pour, they had to hurry back and hang under the tarp to wait out the rain. Filming was taking much longer than I thought it would and I barely had anything recorded at this point. And now we were down a guitarist.

"Maybe there's another way around the traffic," I said hopefully. No one answered me.

I suddenly felt stormy, like the weather. How could things go wrong so quickly? I wasn't filming anything I needed. We were just standing around waiting for the weather to change or a guitar string to arrive. I couldn't just stand here and do nothing! *Think, Z.*

"Guys, we're going to start filming!" I said. Everyone looked at me like I was crazy. "I want to record you guys dancing in the rain. Without raincoats."

"But then we'll get all wet. What about the other shots?" Mari asked from under the nearest tarp. She had been fighting me on the raincoats for this scene all along.

"I wanted to get some footage of you guys dancing in the rain at the end of the video, anyway," I said. "It's only drizzling right now. Come on out and dance it off!" I started to dance around to show them what I meant.

The band members looked skeptically at each other, but one by one they came out from under the tent. Lauren put on some music from her phone, and everyone started to dance. It happened so fast, I didn't have time to think about my shot list, about which camera lens I should use, or whether I should grab a tripod. I just tried to capture the moment. The louder Lauren played the music, the more the band danced.

"That's it!" I told them. "Forget I'm here." The drummer hung back, and I could tell she wasn't thrilled about dancing on camera. "If I can dance like a goofball, you guys can, too!" I said. I handed Mom my camera and busted out my best, most awkward moves, making everyone laugh. I grabbed the camera again and went back to filming. I liked what I was seeing through the viewfinder—a group of friends having a great time in the rain. I filmed a close-up of Mari as she spun around with her eyes closed and then zoomed in on the drummer and the guitarist pretending they were ballroom dancing. I was finally getting something I could use.

I heard a loud rumble of thunder and everyone stopped moving. "No!" I cried as the rain started to come down harder and everyone ran under the tents again. "Not now! We were just getting started!" I yelled at the sky, which responded with another rumble.

We couldn't film outdoors in a thunderstorm. It was too dangerous. Ugh! Why did I ever think this was a good idea? Why?

"Roll with the punches, Z," Mom said gently. "That's what a filmmaker does."

Thanks, Mom, I thought, *but at the moment, it isn't what I want to hear.* The day was failing miserably. "Maybe it will stop soon," I suggested. A crack of thunder and a large flash of lightning said otherwise.

"We should head for cover till this storm passes," Dad said. "Let's get everyone in the cars."

Everyone raced to the cars to wait out the storm. Dad jumped in his, and the band, Lauren, and I jumped in Mom's. The band didn't seem bothered at all about the weather. They chatted and laughed in the backseat, while Mom checked the weather on her phone, and I stewed, reviewing my shot list. Lauren leaned over and gave me a hug.

"Maybe it will stop raining the minute the guitarist's mom gets back with the new string," Lauren said. "Actually, wait, we don't want it to stop raining completely, right? Just no more thunder and lightning?" The sound of more thunder rumbled continuously outside.

"I feel like we're wasting time," I said, feeling fidgety. I drew a raindrop in the condensation that was fogging up the window. "I wish we could film something!"

"You got the dancing in the rain part," Lauren said, being optimistic.

I shrugged. It wasn't enough. I'd had a whole day of filming planned.

"Too bad we don't have your laptop with us," Lauren said. "I really want to see the Kit video before our presentation on Monday."

I banged my head on the car window. How could I

have forgotten our presentation was that Monday? Lauren had been asking to come over for days and I'd been so wrapped up in the CloudSong movie, I pushed her off. "I'm sorry. Want to come over today?" On second thought, I was probably going to try to edit some of my movie footage after we got home. "Or maybe tomorrow?"

I watched Lauren pull her wet blonde hair off her face and into a high ponytail in one quick move. "Don't we have some sound to finish? I found some great music I thought we could use."

I bit my lip. "I already did that." Lauren's face fell. "But you should bring yours over and we'll try that, too." I didn't want to add that I had rushed through the music so I could go back to work on my CloudSong stuff.

Lauren smiled. "It's okay. We'll just use yours if it's done already. But I still want to come watch it once before we present." I nodded. "Have you had a chance to read my 'Homework Hacker' script yet?" she asked.

Groan! I had totally forgotten about that, too! "I keep meaning to start it . . ."

Lauren gave me a look. "It's only three pages long . . ."

"Sorry!" I said, my cheeks flushing. "But I *promise* to read it this weekend." I crossed my heart, and Lauren seemed satisfied.

"Bad news," Mom said, turning and looking at me and the rest of the car. "The weather radar indicates that heavy rain will be moving through for the next few hours."

"No!" I cried. "It didn't say that this morning!"

Mom showed me her weather app as proof. "I know, but that's what it's showing now. We're getting the worst of the storm." Mom put her hand on my shoulder. "You should probably call the shoot, Z," she said quietly. "There's no sense in making everyone hang out in the car."

"But . . ." I stalled. I barely shot any of the footage I needed. I wanted my first cut of my movie to be done in a week and a half so I could spend the following three weeks before the deadline fine-tuning the edit. But now that today was a bust, I couldn't imagine making that deadline. I crumpled my video plan up in a ball. "Fine," I said dejectedly.

"Z," Mom started to say, but I turned away.

I knew I shouldn't take it out on Mom, but I was so

mad! I turned to the window and drew a picture of the sun with my finger, right next to the raindrop. "Rain, rain, go away—and come back another day." My circle grew bigger and bigger, giving me a view of the world outside the car window. The rain was practically coming down sideways. I didn't think I was getting sunshine or rainbows anytime soon.

Mari tapped me on the shoulder. "Hey," she said. "I'm sorry about the video. Maybe we can shoot it another day."

"Thanks," I mumbled. "With school and everyone's activities, there's no way there'll be time to make it happen now."

"Maybe not, but I still wanted you to have this." Mari pulled a flash drive out of her pocket. "This is Needles in a Haystack's amazingly awesome version of 'Singin' in the Rain.' We recorded it the other day for you to use for your edit."

I took the flash drive and held it wordlessly.

Mari smiled. "I think we're even going to start performing it at the Beanery. We like it that much! Even if you can't use it in your movie, I want you to have the file. Maybe it will cheer you up."

"Thanks," I said.

I was sure I'd like listening to Mari's song, but it wasn't going to cheer me up. How could it? My first real film shoot had been a bust. I just had to hope it didn't mean my movie would be, too.

Chapter 6

Showtime

I had my notebook open in front of me, balanced on my knees, as Mom edged along the crowded street to school. I had made a list of everything I'd shot so far that I could use in the CloudSong movie, but I still couldn't figure out what footage went where.

Should I open with footage of me in my neighborhood or use some of the stuff I'd gotten at Kite Hill on Sunday? What about trying to squeeze in paddleboarding on Lake Union with Mom, or scrap it and just let the ice cream shop footage run longer? Was there anything from the Beanery I could use? That was the most fun footage I had.

"Start with one scene you love and build your movie around it," Mom had told me the night before, when I was struggling. "Don't forget your vision." I felt like my vision had been washed out by the rain, just like the music video shoot.

I scribbled over my list of footage and then tore up the paper, piling the scraps next to me along with the remains of four other torn-up pieces of paper. I pulled a fresh sheet out of my notebook and felt the car come to a stop. We were in front of the school. I'd run out of time. Again. I looked out the window and saw kids getting off the bus. I could see Lauren pacing in front of the entrance as kids streamed inside the building.

"Thanks for the ride, Mom," I said as I got out of the car.

"See you tonight, sweetie," she answered. "Don't forget to spare some brain cells for school instead of your movie, okay?"

I gave her a little smile. "I promise," I said before heading over to Lauren. "Hey!" I greeted her.

Lauren turned around. Her face was full of worry. "Oh good, you're here! When you didn't text me back this morning, and then I didn't see you get off the bus, I thought you were sick."

"Sorry," I apologized. "I was trying to cut some of my footage before I got the bus this morning and completely forgot to turn on my phone. Everything okay?"

Lauren hiked her backpack higher on her shoulders. A neon-yellow soccer ball hung from the back. "Yeah, I just wish we could have gotten together once this weekend to watch the presentation again."

I felt a pang of guilt. I'd really left Lauren flat this weekend. "I know, I was going to call you, but we were all so tired after the shoot on Saturday, and Sunday I didn't realize my parents were taking me hiking so we weren't home," I said. "But I promise our video is going to be the best thing Mr. Kozak has ever seen. Trust me."

"Okay." Lauren shrugged. "I trust you. You have the flash drive, right?"

I pulled the flash drive out of the front pocket of my bag and held it up for her to see. "I checked three times to make sure I brought it."

"Good." Lauren pushed her blonde hair out of her eyes and exhaled slowly. "I think Mr. Kozak said we're up first."

I threw my arm around Lauren. "If you get nervous, just look at me and I'll make a face like this." I stuck my tongue out and rolled my eyes, then shimmied around. Lauren started to laugh. "Do you think Mr. Kozak will notice?"

"Possibly," Lauren said, loosening up. "But when he sees how good our project is, I'm sure he won't mind."

I kept it going. "I bet he grades us an 'E' for 'Emmy-worthy.'"

"Now you're going too far," Lauren said as the first bell rang.

We had only three minutes to get to class so we rushed into school and upstairs to social studies on the second floor. Kids were chatting and getting their books out. I gave Lauren a thumbs-up and headed straight to Mr. Kozak to give him my flash drive. He put it into his computer and began setting up the file for the SMART Board. He pulled up my drive for me, and I scrolled until I found the file labeled FINALCALI-RUSH. Then I went back to my seat to wait for class to start.

I glanced at Lauren as Mr. Kozak called attendance. She looked worried again, so I made my eyebrows go up and down and flashed her a goofy grin. She finally cracked a smile.

"Let's call up our first two presenters, Lauren and Z, to give their report on the California gold rush," Mr. Kozak said to the class. "They did something unique for their presentation—a video."

I smiled at Lauren as we walked to the front of the class. Lauren headed to the right of the SMART Board while I stepped to the left to recite our short opening. Andrew gave me a thumbs-up from his seat.

"Lauren and I were assigned the California gold rush," I told the class, "but instead of doing a verbal presentation, we thought we'd put our own spin on the project and make a stop-motion video to really *show* you the history."

I pressed PLAY, and the title appeared. Lauren had edited this part, and it looked fantastic, like an old silent movie opening. It was black and white with the words CALIFORNIA GOLD RUSH in a jumpy print. Then the movie faded into view.

"Hi, I'm Kit!" Lauren's voice-over started with an image of my Kit doll standing in front of the papier-mâché mountain. "And I'm here to—"

The movie jumped to a clip of Mari's band playing at the Beanery.

"One-two-three-four!" Mari shouted in the clip and started to play.

The class looked confused, and Lauren and I looked at each other panicked.

Where was our California gold rush video?

I darted back to the computer to see if I'd clicked on the wrong file. "We just need a second," I said to Mr. Kozak, my palms beginning to sweat. "I must have opened the wrong video. Let me find the right one."

"What's going on?" Lauren whispered. "Where is the video?"

"It's got to be on here," I whispered back, but my heart was pumping. I scrolled through the files again. The only one that said FINAL on it was the one I'd opened. Maybe it was under an older title? I clicked on another video that said CALIFORNIA GOLD RUSH and a silent version of the same opening began to play.

"Z, where is it?" Lauren said urgently. "You said you checked."

"I did!" I whispered back. I clicked on another clip that said the word RUSH. A video of Popcorn racing around my room with a squeaky movie popcorn box began to play. Everyone laughed, and I quickly shut it off. I could feel my cheeks burn. I looked at Lauren's and hers was equally red. So were her eyes—I could see tears starting to well up. I couldn't blame her for being upset. This was all my fault.

"Mr. Kozak, I'm so sorry," I said shakily. "I must have grabbed the wrong flash drive this morning."

Mr. Kozak wrote something in his notebook. Was he deducting points off our grade for this?

"I'll give you a pass today, ladies," he said, and I audibly exhaled. "But you should be ready to present on Friday."

"Thank you," I said for the two of us. Lauren was quiet. "I promise I'll bring the right file in. We can even go tomorrow."

"I'm sorry, Z, but that wouldn't be fair to the other students scheduled for tomorrow," Mr. Kozak said. "I can't bump them because you weren't prepared today."

I made eye contact with Maddie. She gave me a sympathetic look. I'd embarrassed Lauren and myself in front of the whole class. "We understand," I said, and Lauren nodded. "Thank you. We'll be ready on Friday."

I tried to get Lauren's attention after we sat back down, but she wouldn't look my way. I barely heard Maddie and her partner present on the building of the Brooklyn Bridge. All I could think about was our video. Could I have accidentally deleted it? Was our movie gone? My heart started to beat faster. No, it had to be on my hard drive. I just messed up. Big-time. When the bell rang, Lauren was the first one out the door. I rushed after her to our lockers.

"I don't know what happened," I said, but Lauren still wouldn't look at me. "The last time I watched the video, it was all on there. I must have given it a new file name or something. I know it's at home on my hard drive." Lauren didn't say anything. "We'll present on Friday and everything will be fine. I don't think Mr. Kozak will take any points off."

"I hope not," Lauren said quietly. "I need a good grade on this. I didn't do very well on the last test." Her face was scrunched up tight. "It's just . . . this is important, and it doesn't seem like you care. The CloudSong Film Festival is not the only thing going on in the world, you know."

Ouch. I felt like I'd been hit in the stomach. "I know that," I said quickly.

"Really?" Lauren asked, shoving some books around her locker instead of looking at me. "So that means you read my 'Homework Hacker' script?" I looked down at my sneakers. "See?"

I tried to change the subject. "Why don't you come over today and we'll find the Kit video together? We can put in the song you suggested, too." I felt panicked. Lauren and I never fought. I'd really screwed up.

The *Real* Z

Lauren's blue eyes were super stormy. "No, thanks. I have plans with some of the soccer team after school. Besides, it's not like you need me. You edited most of the movie yourself anyway." Lauren shut her locker and walked away down the crowded hallway.

"I feel awful!" I told Mariela when we scootered home together after school. "I don't think Mr. Kozak is going to take off any points on our project, but Lauren is still really mad at me."

"Do you blame her?" Mari asked.

"No, but it was an accident," I said miserably.

"Did you tell her you were sorry?" Mari asked.

I tried to remember if the words "I'm sorry" ever came out of my mouth. I wasn't sure they had. "She didn't really want to talk to me the rest of the day. We didn't speak at Camera Club, either. All she said to me was that I had taken over the whole project and the only thing I could think about was CloudSong." We scootered to a stop and waited for the light to change. I looked at Mari. Her lips were pursed.

"You do talk about CloudSong a lot," Mari said finally.

"That's because it's a big deal," I said, getting worked up. "It's a film festival. I need my movie to be perfect if I want any shot at winning. And if I win, I was going to use the money to buy Camera Club a new camera. The one we used for filming broke."

"That sounds like a big deal, but it doesn't mean you can just ignore everything else, Z," Mari said tentatively. "Lauren was really excited about this project, and you pushed it aside like it didn't matter."

"Wait, did she talk to you?" I asked accusingly.

Mari nodded. "She was really upset."

"Well, so am I!" I said. "Now I have to spend more time finishing this social studies project instead of working on my movie. A movie that isn't coming together. All I have is an arrangement of a silly song and a bunch of scenes that don't go together."

"A silly song?" Mari repeated gruffly. "I thought you liked the arrangement we did."

"I do!" Uh-oh. I had put my foot in my mouth again. I fumbled for the right words. "That's not what I mean. I just . . . Nothing is working out the way it's supposed to. I wanted to be done with my first cut by now and—"

"You know what, Z?" Mari said. "I think Lauren is right. CloudSong is all you care about right now."

I immediately regretted my words. "That's not true. Mari, I'm sorry. I didn't mean it like that." We crossed the street and scootered down the block, Mari keeping a little ahead of me. She didn't say anything as we came to a stop in front of our houses.

"Hi, girls!" Dad called out, and I looked over in bewilderment. I hadn't seen him weeding in the front yard. "Z, ready to head down to the Locks to film?"

I was so distracted by what happened with Lauren, I forgot we'd planned that for today. "Uh, yeah," I said, glancing at Mari. "But could Mari and I have a quick snack together first? We've got to talk about something."

"Sure!" Dad called back. "I just made the meanest batch of chocolate chip muffins."

"Thank you, Mr. Yang, but I have to get home," Mari said stiffly, and scootered off without even saying good-bye. Dad gave me a questioning look, but I shrugged and rushed inside.

It was the second time in the same day that I had watched one of my friends leave in a huff. It wasn't a good feeling.

Chapter 7

Total Pro

Here we go," I said as Dad and I watched the small drone take flight like a super expensive paper airplane.

But even as I was flying it, all I could think about was Lauren and Mari. *I can't believe how mad they got*, I thought to myself as I used the remote to take the drone higher to get a good view. *Lauren and Mari are wrong. I do not only think about my CloudSong movie!*

"Z!" Dad shouted. "You're going to hit the top of that boat!"

I was so worked up, I wasn't paying attention to where the drone was headed!

I quickly snapped out of my thoughts and navigated the drone higher, around the top of the sail boat mast. Whoa, that was close. "It's okay," I said.

"Be careful," Dad warned me.

"I know," I grumbled. I knew Dad wasn't totally

supportive of my spending so much of my grant money on renting the drone. He thought it was a waste, but Becka had seemed so sure that a drone would make my footage look edgy. Mom and I watched a few videos filmed with drones, and they looked really unique. That's what I was going for with these shots. Now I just hoped I got some good footage.

The drone rose higher and higher before I sent it over the water toward the Hiram M. Chittenden Locks. A ton of people visit the Locks each year to watch boats and ships get raised and lowered at different water levels along the river and canal waterways at the west end of Salmon Bay. I loved watching the boats go through the channels and watching the salmon swim upstream. Dad said I used to beg to take one home as a pet!

"Look at that drone go!" marveled Dad as we watched the machine zoom along, becoming a tiny dot on the horizon. People walking on the docks looked up as they heard a faint buzzing sound over their heads.

I turned my attention back to the handheld device that controlled the drone, looking at the screen that showed me the footage the drone was taking. I had studied the drone manual carefully—I didn't want to break it!—and I knew how far it could go and what to do if the drone went out of range, but I still wasn't sure how the footage would look in my movie. I looked at the screen again and frowned. Uh-oh. So far the only thing the drone was recording was choppy water.

"How does the video look?" Dad asked me.

"It looks cool!" I said unconvincingly. I knew the truth—my recording of the Locks looked . . . dull. Even as a large shipping boat and the channels finally came into view, it was still boring.

Dad leaned over my shoulder and looked at the screen. "Huh. All I see is water."

"It's pretty water," I countered, my heart pounding. I didn't want Dad to know I was having doubts about renting the drone. I needed something to go right today. "I just need to get closer."

"Can you do that?" Dad asked.

I stopped paying attention to the drone and looked at him. "What do you mean?"

"Z," Dad said, sounding slightly impatient. "I told

you to look up whether you could fly the drone over a public place like this. There are laws. Didn't you look up the rules for this area?"

"I forgot," I said without thinking, and Dad looked at me. "I'm sorry! I've been really busy between homework and filming and . . ." *And the CloudSong movie*, I thought, hearing Mari in my head. *Ugh!* Maybe my friends were right, but I couldn't think about that now.

Was this drone footage going to be a bust, too? I threw back my head, frustrated. "It's not a big deal. I'm not doing anything dangerous with the drone."

"Z, there are rules for flying a drone," he repeated. "Mom and I talked to you about that. If you haven't done your research, I'm sorry, but you should bring the drone in."

"Fine," I said stubbornly, and started to bring the drone back. I was annoyed with Dad, but secretly I knew he was right. I was so anxious about how my movie was going to fit together that I hadn't done my homework checking out whether I could fly a drone here.

But even if I had, I kind of knew this footage wasn't

working for me. Sure, the water was a gorgeous shade of amber in spots where the setting sun reflected off it, but I wasn't going to get a good shot of that now.

"You're right," I said with a sigh. "I'm sorry I got mad at you. I just had a rough day and wanted so badly to get some footage I could use."

"Want to talk about it?" Dad's expression softened. I shook my head. I was afraid if I did, I might get upset in public. "Okay, well, why don't you use your regular camera down here instead?" Dad suggested.

That was a good idea! I landed the drone safely on the docks and carefully put it back in its carrying bag, then took out my trusty camera. I wasn't really sure what footage I would get, but Mom always said, *Trust your gut.* That's what I would do.

"Mr. Production Assistant?" I joked, referring to Dad. He had been calling himself that since we got in the car and headed downtown that afternoon. "Will you still work for me even though I got mad before?"

Dad smiled. "Of course, director. At your service. What would you like me to do?"

"Let's walk all the way to the edge of this dock

and get some video close-up of the salmon." I pointed down the walkway. "And maybe we can take one home as a pet."

Dad laughed. "Here we go again. We'll talk about it. To the Locks!" he declared and ran ahead. I followed, and instinctively pulled my phone out of my pocket to send Lauren a text to share about the drone disaster.

> **z:** Hey! At the Locks and almost crashed the drone. So distracted. LOL.

I waited a few seconds to see if Lauren would respond. She didn't. Maybe she was at soccer practice. Oh, wait. Didn't she say she was doing something with some of the girls on the team after school? Was she reading my text and ignoring it? My stomach tightened. I had made the text all about my filming again—probably not the smartest move. I tried again.

> **z:** Can't wait for our presentation on Friday. We will nail it, then we can work on "The Homework Hacker"!

That time I could see the little ball spinning at the bottom of the text, like Lauren was responding. But nothing popped up. If she was texting with someone, it wasn't me. I shoved my phone back in my pocket. Trying to push Lauren and our fight out of my mind, I set my camera to record and followed after Dad. I soaked in the view—the Locks lifting boats up and down in the water, close-ups of the Locks themselves, the boats floating by, and tourists taking pictures of the sunset. I loved watching people enjoy my city as much as I did. Hmm . . . maybe I could put on my reporter hat like I did for Camera Club. Adding a few Seattleite characters would give this movie some color. I fished around in my messenger bag for my small pocket recorder, then scanned the area for interesting interview subjects.

"Excuse me?" I asked a couple with a red-headed toddler who was eagerly pointing to the water. I cleared my throat—it was a little nerve-racking interviewing complete strangers. "Do you maybe have a minute to answer some questions on camera? I'm making a documentary about Seattle."

"Sure!" the woman answered.

"Okay, great—thanks. What brought you to the Locks today?"

"Our son loves looking at the fish, and this is so much better than Pike Place Market where the fish are already"—the woman made a face, and then used air quotes in front of the little boy—"sleeping."

I laughed. "So you come here all the time?"

"We like to take weekly walks down here to see the fish and the boats," the dad explained. "Right, Deacon?"

Deacon, the red-headed toddler, seemed too young to talk, but he pointed to the water and giggled every time he saw a salmon swim by under the water. His mom held his hand tightly. I knelt down to Deacon's level, and he eyed my camera gear with interest.

"You like the fish, buddy?" I asked, and the kid's face lit up. He kept pointing to the water. I looked up at his parents and asked, "What would you say Seattle means to your family?"

"Home," the mom said without hesitating. "I can't imagine living anywhere else."

"Even somewhere with less rain?" Deacon's dad teased.

"The rainy days just make the sunny days we have that much more special," the mom said.

Bingo. I loved that line. I had to make sure I used that footage in my movie.

I thanked the parents and waved good-bye to Deacon before making my way farther down the docks to find Dad. He was standing near the fish ladder, an area of the Locks with a tunnel-like opening that the salmon swam through. At the end of the twenty-one openings in the ladder, the salmon broke free into the fresh water of Salmon Bay. The salmon work so hard to swim up through the ladder. Working on this project was beginning to make me feel like those salmon. I felt like I was swimming and swimming and getting nowhere. With my friends, with this movie, with my school project.

"Do you want to head home so you can shoot some more footage with the drone before sunset?" Dad asked me.

I shook my head. "It's okay. I can film it tomorrow," I told Dad.

"Okay," Dad said, staring out at the water. I looked at him in his favorite Mariners tee and a baseball cap from one of Mom's film shoots. He'd hurried home from work to help me and I had been super cranky with him. I tucked myself under his arm. "Thanks again for taking me filming today," I said quietly.

"Of course," Dad said, squeezing my arm. "I know you've got a lot on your mind. I hope you don't forget an important part of doing all this, though, is having fun."

"I know," I said. I was getting so frustrated with everyone and everything I was forgetting to enjoy myself. Entering my first film contest was hard, but it was supposed to be exciting, too. "I'll try to have more fun," I vowed.

"That's my girl," Dad said.

I looked out at the water and wondered what Lauren and Mari were doing. The sun was dipping lower, and I'd never seen the Seattle sky look more like a postcard. I tucked my camera back into my bag.

"Don't you want to film this?" Dad asked as Popcorn took a seat on my feet like she always did when I finally stood still. It was like she didn't want us to move, either. "That's a gorgeous sunset."

I smiled. "It is. But I don't want to give away all of

Seattle's secrets," I said. "Let's keep this one for you and me."

Dad hugged me back. "I'd like that."

Then we both turned and watched in silence as the sun slowly sank below the water, taking the last rays of sunlight with it.

Chapter 8

Rainy Week Blues

It rained for the next two days straight.

In a city as rainy as Seattle, people just put on their rain boots, grab a raincoat and umbrella, and keep moving. Me? I didn't want to go anywhere.

I was fighting with my two best friends in the world. Neither of them were speaking to me. Lauren ignored me in class and at Camera Club, and Mariela had scootered home without me. Even thinking about helping Camera Club get a new camera didn't cheer me up. Nothing felt as fun if I didn't have my friends to share it with.

I lay on my bed and listened to the sound of rain hitting the roof. I was too frustrated to edit my movie. Instead, I pulled "The Horrible Homework Hacker" out of my folder and finally read Lauren's script. As Popcorn snuggled beside me, I laughed out loud at her story. I was done reading in five minutes. *Five minutes* I could never find before. My stomach twisted into a knot from guilt. I tried texting Lauren again:

z: LOVE "The Homework Hacker" script!

For the umpteenth time that week, she didn't respond. I threw my phone across the bed, startling Popcorn.

"Sorry, girl," I said, and scratched her behind the ears. At least Popcorn wasn't mad at me. I looked up. The bulletin board that hung next to my bed caught my eye. My favorite picture of me with Lauren, eating cotton candy at a Seattle street fair, stared back at me. I missed my best friend.

I heard a knock at my door.

"Very late production assistant reporting for duty," Dad said. He had been working downstairs on a prototype for a new plane, and Mom was at the university grading a big exam. Popcorn jumped off the bed and ran straight toward him.

"It's okay," I said. I was going to make a joke about Dad being fired, but my heart wasn't in it. "I've shut the set down today."

"Shut down the set?" Dad asked, sitting down on the edge of my bed. "Are you on strike?"

I shook my head yes, then shook my head no. "I'm just not in the mood to film today."

"Everything okay?" Dad asked, growing serious.

"Lauren and Mari are mad at me," I said. I could feel my lower lip start to quiver.

"Ah, is this why you were so upset at the Locks the other day?" Dad asked.

I sat up. "Yes." I was dying to tell someone what was going on. Gigi was traveling, and Becka had a wheelchair basketball tournament. I liked Andrew and Maddie, but I didn't want to make them feel like they had to pick sides. There was no one around to talk to with Mari and Lauren not speaking to me. So I spilled my guts to Dad.

"It sounds like you really hurt Mari's feelings," Dad said. "Have you apologized?"

"Well, not exactly, but . . . ," I protested. "They both said all I've been talking about is CloudSong and nothing else."

"Well, haven't you?" Dad asked honestly.

"Well, maybe, but this is a huge deal," I reminded him.

"It is," Dad agreed, "but so is the social studies project. Lauren worked hard on it and she wanted to be more involved, and it sounds like you didn't let her."

I thought back to how many times she had asked to help and I had shut her down. And it had taken me till today to read her script for our next AGSM.

"And Mari and her band took time out of their practices to record a version of the song you wanted in your movie. How do you think she felt, hearing you act like that was no big deal?" Dad asked.

Well, when he put it that way. . .

I flopped down on my bed again. Maybe my friends were right: I was living, breathing, and talking about the CloudSong movie 24-7. I had forgotten to pay attention to everything else around me. I had made Mari feel like her music didn't matter and let Lauren think our project wasn't important.

"I'm a bad friend," I said, pulling down my beanie over my face.

Dad patted me on the back. "Everyone makes mistakes. The important thing about being a *good* friend is knowing how to apologize. They'll come around."

"I've been calling and texting them for days," I said miserably.

"Have you tried apologizing in person?" Dad asked. "You know, the old-fashioned way, not on a screen. Saying sorry face-to-face?"

I sat up. "No," I admitted. Dad and Popcorn both looked at me. If I wanted to make things right, I needed to show my friends how much they meant to me. "You're right." I glanced at the clock. It was 5:45. "Do I have some time before dinner? Maybe I'll take Popcorn for a walk and stop by Mari's."

The word "walk" was all Popcorn had to hear. She started barking and ran to my door.

"Sure," Dad said. "We're getting takeout, and I haven't even ordered yet. You have plenty of time."

Just knowing I was going to talk to Mari made me feel a little brighter. I grabbed my camera—just in case. I never knew when inspiration was going to strike. I also took my Windbreaker from the downstairs closet and put on Popcorn's leash, rain hat, and booties. It was drizzling, and I wanted to be prepared if the sky opened up.

When we stepped onto the porch, I stood there for a moment, letting the cool air hit my face. My eyes immediately scanned to Mari's house next door. Her mom's car was parked out front, so I hoped that meant Mari was home, too. We walked straight to her front door, Popcorn tugging on her leash. I hesitated for half a second and then knocked. Two seconds later, Mari came to the door. When she saw me her smile faded, and she looked down at her sneakers. She was wearing one black high-top lace-up and one bright pink one.

"I know you're mad at me and you have every right to be," I said with a shaky voice "I said something stupid and I didn't mean it. I'm so grateful to you and your band for doing a song arrangement just for me. I love it."

"Thanks, Z," Mari said. I couldn't really tell what Mari was feeling, so I went on.

"Friends are also supposed to make you feel good about yourself, not bad," I said quietly. "I'm so sorry I hurt your feelings."

Mari grabbed my hand and gave it a squeeze. "It's okay. I knew that you didn't really mean it, but yeah, you're right, it did hurt my feelings."

I squeezed her hand back. "Thanks for keeping me honest," I said with a little laugh.

"What are friends for?" She pulled me in for a hug.

Resolving things with Mari made me want to run

over to Lauren's house right away, but I knew she had a soccer game. And besides, I knew I had to do more than just apologize to Lauren. I had to show her that I really cared about our friendship, even though I hadn't been acting like it the last few weeks. The question was: how?

Maybe I'd think of something on my walk with Popcorn. The two of us walked quietly down the block listening to the sounds of my neighborhood—car tires splashing through puddles, birds coming out after a storm, the McManus kids skateboarding down their long driveway, a mother talking on her cell phone while her baby babbled in her stroller. Popcorn took her usual turn onto Plum Street, and I saw Mrs. Tollman gardening.

Most people in our neighborhood had their gardens in the back, but the Tollmans' front yard was huge and everyone in the area loved to look at their gardening boxes, which were always full of watermelon, zucchini, and even pumpkins in the fall. I watched Mrs. Tollman till the dirt that would soon grow into thriving plants that always reminded me of a forest.

"Hi, Z," Mrs. Tollman greeted me as I approached.

"Are you and Popcorn getting in a walk before it pours again?"

"Yes. I see you're starting your garden."

"I've been waiting weeks to plant," she told me. "I have French string beans this year and am even trying to grow brussels sprouts. We'll see how that goes."

If Dad and I had a question about growing a garden, Mrs. Tollman always had the answer. If someone was in need of a tomato or a zucchini for a recipe, the Tollmans were the first people anyone asked. Everyone in our community knew the Tollmans. They were like family. *Family.* Hmm . . . I could feel an idea brewing! "Could you tell me a bit about your garden for a movie I'm working on?" I asked.

"Sure!" Mrs. Tollman touched her hair. "I've always wanted to be in a movie."

I pulled out my tiny voice recorder and turned on my camera. Then I started filming as Mrs. Tollman talked about the right time to plant seeds versus tiny plants and how to know when to water and how much sunlight was needed for a garden to grow. I zoomed in on Mrs. Tollman's gardening gloves, then shot the tiny vegetable signs she had placed where plants would soon grow. I filmed her straightening her large gardening hat, her face barely visible under the large visor.

She looked at the dirt patch that would someday turn into a garden. "You know, some people think starting a garden is too much work, but I love a challenge." She smiled. "What's that saying? The tougher the problem, the greater the reward? I believe that."

I thought of my fight with Lauren. Admitting I was wrong was scary. I realized now how wrong I had been. I had to show Lauren that her ideas and the things she loved were as important to me as what was going on in my own life.

I glanced at the time on my phone. Lauren would be at her soccer game, which was just starting. Maybe I could catch her there.

"Thanks for talking to me," I said to Mrs. Tollman, "and good luck with your garden." Then I pulled on Popcorn's leash. "Let's get you home," I said, and started to run down the block with her nipping at my heels.

I flew through the front door and went straight to Mom and Dad who were in the kitchen. It didn't take me long to explain what I wanted to do. Since Dad was the one who suggested I talk to my friends face-to-face anyway, he was fine with dropping me off at Lauren's game and keeping my dinner warm (it hadn't even arrived yet).

"I just need five minutes," I said, running upstairs with an idea pounding in my head. I grabbed some giant pieces of poster board that I always had ready for backdrops, then went to the bag of candy still sitting on my dresser from Lauren and my last trip to Sweet Treats, the candy shop in town. Then I grabbed a bottle of quick-drying glue that Lauren always used when we were making AGSM props. I quickly got to work. I walked downstairs carefully, holding the large poster board flat so that nothing would slide off it as it dried. Dad took a look.

"Perfect," he said.

"Good luck," Mom said, hugging me carefully to avoid wrecking the poster. "Just be honest and tell her how you feel."

"I will," I promised.

Dad drove me back to school and let me off near the soccer field. The game was already going, and there were some fans sitting up in the bleachers, but not as many as usual. The earlier rain had kept people away. I pulled my Windbreaker hood around my head and carefully pulled the poster board out of the back of our truck.

Dad rolled down the window. "I'll pick you up here in an hour, but call me if it starts raining and you want me to get you sooner."

"Okay," I said.

I was suddenly nervous. What if Lauren saw me on the sidelines during the game and got annoyed? Or became distracted and missed a goal that cost them the game? I had to at least try to explain. I took a deep breath and started walking. By the time I reached the actual field, it had started drizzling again. I looked at the scoreboard. It was 1–0 in our school's favor and close to the end of the first half.

Right away, I spotted Lauren running down the field in our school's green-and-white soccer uniform, keeping the ball away from the opposing team. I took a seat in the first row of the bleachers and watched as Lauren pulled the soccer ball back with her foot and scooted around a girl on the other team. Then Lauren broke away from the pack and kicked the ball down the field. As a striker, she usually scored a lot of goals, and I had a feeling she was about to score one now.

"Go, Pine Crest!" someone behind me shouted, screaming our middle school's name.

"Go, Lauren!" I screamed at the top of my lungs as Lauren punted the ball.

I felt like I was watching the game in slow motion. I watched the ball sail through the air and the goalie on the other team try to block it. The goalie jumped, her hands over her head, but the ball flew higher than her outstretched arms and landed in the net. Score!

I jumped up and cheered along with the other fans. The buzzer sounded, ending the first period, and Lauren ran off the field to the bench. I watched her high-five her teammates. That's when I held up my sign. Then I took a deep breath.

"Lauren!" I shouted. She immediately looked up to see who was yelling her name. Her face registered surprise when she saw my sign. I held it higher. I had written out the words, *"The Horrible Homework Hacker," an AGSM original coming soon from Lauren and Z!* in candy gummies and chocolates. Beneath it, in marker, I'd written: *I'M SORRY!* Lauren's mouth turned up into a smile.

She walked over to the fence. "Come see me after the game," she said. She smiled a little. "That is, if you don't have too much work to do on CloudSong to stay and watch."

"I'm staying," I said.

I sat back down with my sign. It was a really good game. Pine Crest Middle School wound up winning 6–4, and Lauren scored three goals. I cheered, shouted, and shimmied as Lauren tore up the field. I knew she was fast, but I hadn't realized how much faster she'd gotten since last year. The season had started only a few weeks ago, and I had been so busy, I hadn't come to see Lauren play yet. Meanwhile, she'd given up her Saturday to help me shoot a video. When the game was over, I waited for Lauren in the bleachers.

"Hey," I said awkwardly. My hands were sweaty and my mouth felt dry. I wanted to say the right thing for once. "You should win team MVP. You were amazing out there."

"Thanks," Lauren said quietly. "It was great of you to come to the game."

"I'm going to come to more of them," I said. "That's what best friends do." I felt my throat tighten. "They also know when they've royally screwed up. I'm sorry I made you feel like your ideas for our project didn't matter." Lauren scuffed her cleats on the muddy grass and didn't respond. "You kept asking to help edit, and I just ignored you. That was wrong. So was not reading your script. You helped me with my movie. I should have cared more about what you wanted to work on, too."

Lauren shrugged. "I know making movies is your thing, but it really hurt when you kept telling me you didn't need my help with our social studies project. And then when the presentation was missing from the flash drive, you kind of acted like it was no big deal. But it was to me. I need a good grade on that project." Lauren looked upset again.

"I know how important it is for you to get good grades," I said. "That's why I'm going to tell Mr. Kozak again in class tomorrow that this was all my fault. He should know you were prepared and I wasn't."

"Thanks," Lauren said, and sort of smiled. "Look, I know I'm good on the field, but when we're in class, sometimes facts get jumbled in my head. I understand them better when we're working together. Plus, I *like* making stuff with you."

"I do, too," I assured her. "I know our presentation comes first, but then do you want to start working on 'The Horrible Homework Hacker'? The script is really good. I seriously LOL'ed."

Lauren's smile widened. "Thanks. That sounds awesome." She touched the poster. "Let's do something like this for our title treatment."

I looked at the poster again. "Good idea!"

"Too bad you wasted all that perfectly good candy," Lauren teased, perking up.

"I can always get more candy," I said, "but I can't replace my best friend."

"Aww," Lauren said as she dramatically pretended to wipe away a tear. "This is like a scene in a movie."

"Yes! I think this is the part where we're supposed to hug before the scene fades out," I said.

We looked at each other, then yelled at the same time, "HUG!" and collapsed into laughter.

Chapter 9

Sneak Peek

Lauren and I pushed open the classroom door to the crowded hallway and let out the sound we'd been holding in for fifteen minutes.

Squeeeee!

The two of us jumped up and down.

"Mr. Kozak loved it! He actually used the word 'love,'" Lauren said in awe.

"We did it," I said. "Together."

Lauren smiled. "Yes we did!"

Lauren had come over Thursday after school, and we'd ended up changing the instrumental music (Lauren's option *was* better) and cutting a quick scene that felt out of place. Her suggestions were great—I should have been listening to them all along. A good director, I was learning, could take criticism.

Lauren bounced on her toes. "We have to celebrate! I don't have soccer practice until five thirty today."

"Okay," I said, happy that Lauren and I were hanging out again. "Where should we go?"

I looked out the window. The sun was peeking through the clouds, and the weather was just the way I liked it—warm but not sticky. "How about Sweet Treats? I've been wanting to try their watermelon coconut smoothie, and they have it for only a few weeks a year. I can ask my dad if he can drop us off after school."

"Perfect!" Lauren said.

That afternoon, Lauren and I ordered the watermelon coconut smoothie with sprinkles and whipped cream topping. Lauren took a long sip of her icy drink, coming up with a smoothie mustache. I started to laugh and snapped a picture with my phone.

"What's so funny?" Lauren asked.

"You've got a mustache," I said, and showed her the picture. She started to laugh, too, then made funny faces.

"Oh, I've got to film this," I said, holding up my phone to record. I hesitated. "Do you mind?"

"Nope," Lauren said, and made another mustache. She was acting like a total goofball. "This smoothie is amazing. Might be their best."

"I'm not sure," I said, and turned the camera on

myself. "I also like the Strawberry Who-Are-You-Calling-Short? Cake Smoothie."

Lauren laughed so hard she hiccupped. "You made that flavor up! I've never heard of that!"

"Maybe," I answered. "But you have to admit it would be a great flavor!"

Filming the two of us was so much fun. I liked having a record of things that made me happy. And I wasn't thinking about my CloudSong movie at all. We didn't even talk about it once. And that was okay.

That evening, pumped up by my afternoon (and sugary smoothie) with Lauren, I took a new look at my documentary. I put sticky notes representing all the footage I had on my whiteboard and moved them around in different combinations, figuring out how they fit together. Where was the story?

Maybe the Locks could lead into the walking shot, and . . . hmmm. That could actually work! I moved some more sticky notes around, writing script ideas on a notepad as I went.

By the time Mom popped her head in to tell me it was time for bed, I'd put together a rough cut. I looked at the calendar—I still had four weeks to perfect the edit. I needed to do my title treatment and my credits and add in some music, but I thought the footage looked great. Especially the part where Mari's band danced in the rain and I played their version of "Singin' in the Rain." I couldn't wait for her to see it.

I sent off a quick e-mail to my friends:

> Anyone want to see a sneak preview of my movie tomorrow morning? Popcorn's on me! (No, really, she's sitting on me. It's super hard to type this.)

Everyone responded excitedly, so we'd decided on 10 a.m. Mari and Lauren would come over and we'd video chat with Gigi and Becka.

When I heard the doorbell ring the next morning, I jumped up and shouted, "It's movie premiere time!"

Lauren and Mari came running up the stairs and burst into my bedroom. Mari was carrying a small bouquet of sunflowers, and Lauren had a roll of red paper. I watched her stretch it out onto the floor.

"It's your first red carpet," Lauren said triumphantly.

I strutted up and down the paper walkway as Lauren and Mari cheered, snapping pictures with their phones. Popcorn looked on in bewilderment.

"I can't wait for you guys to see the film," I said. "I think it's really coming along."

"We can't wait, either!" Lauren said. "It's like we're watching an exclusive director's cut."

We all laughed and I walked over to my computer to make sure the video chat window was open. Gigi and Becka waved back at me.

"Hi, guys! Are you ready?" I asked. "You got the e-mail attachment of the video and it's loaded? I want you all to see it at the same time."

"All good here!" Becka said.

"Ready in London, too!" said Gigi, who was now home again for a few weeks.

"Okay, then," I said as Lauren and Mari gathered around my laptop. I pretended to play the trumpet to announce my movie. Then I opened the large playback window and saw my video on pause. "And three-two-one! Press PLAY!"

I sat back with Mari and Lauren and watched. I had decided to arrange the footage from sunrise to sunset with the rain storm with Mari's band at the end. The movie opened with a shot of the sun and drone footage of my house—a bird's-eye view of my world. Then I took viewers through a day in Seattle. Some parts were scenes from my life and some scenes featured my city. I loved the footage I shot of Mari while we scootered to school and the scene with Lauren in Sweet Treats from the previous day. I kept in the footage of the Locks—when it was all cut together, it was beautiful. I also experimented with some grainy shots and ones in sharp focus. There were quick shots of famous landmarks and a segment where I interviewed the couple with the toddler on the docks. When I wasn't doing an interview on camera, I stuck with some instrumental music Mari had given me from her band. I was considering adding a voice-over that played over the course of the whole movie, like I do on my vlog, but then I read an article online about how continuous voice-overs were distracting. Plus, I wanted my film to speak for itself. Next, I included footage of

Mari's band playing at the Beanery. But the best part was the rain dance at the end with Needles in a Haystack. As we watched, the three of us were rocking out to Mari's group's song arrangement of "Singin' in the Rain" in my bedroom. This was starting to feel like a real movie! I ended with an image of the sun coming out from behind a cloud and setting on the city, and finally the last shot was of me standing on my front porch again, slowly waving good-bye as the sun began to set. As the screen faded to black, Mari and Lauren applauded. Becka whistled and Gigi cheered.

"Take a bow!" Gigi shouted.

I stood up in front of the computer screen and bowed to Becka and Gigi and then curtsied to Mari and Lauren. "So . . . what did you guys think?" I asked eagerly.

"*Great* cinematography," Becka said.

"I can't believe you included the milk mustache," Lauren added. "That was funny."

"I liked that part the best," Mari added. "Well, that and the part of everyone dancing in the rain. I didn't think you got anything worth using that day, but that part looked cool and I loved hearing the song in the movie. Hey, my song is in a movie!"

"That was the best part in the film," Gigi said, and the others nodded. "I wish you had more scenes like that."

"Me, too," Lauren said. "That scene felt very you, very Z."

"Yeah!" Becka agreed. "Some of the other scenes felt like they were someone else's movie."

I paused. Uh-oh. That didn't sound good. "What do you mean?" I asked, grabbing my notebook to take notes.

Everyone got kind of quiet. "Come on, guys, I need your help! If you don't tell me what to fix, how can I make my movie better?" *Good filmmakers take criticism,* I reminded myself, remembering how valuable Lauren's insight had been for our Kit video. I could handle my friends' comments.

Hopefully.

"I didn't *not* like anything," Lauren said carefully. "Does that make sense?" She turned to Mari for confirmation. "It's just . . . all the pieces were nice, but . . . I don't know. I wasn't sure if they all fit together."

"Yes, that's it!" Gigi exclaimed. "The movie was missing a story."

My stomach lurched. My movie still didn't have a story? That was the most important part of a movie! "But

I told the story of the city from sun up to sun down," I reminded them. "You know all those shots of the sun and the rain throughout the day . . ." I trailed off.

"I got that," Becka said, "but it didn't feel like a movie really made by you. Some parts of the movie felt like you made them, like the part with the smoothies, but other parts were pretty but kind of, well, dull like a travel commercial."

"That's a good way to put it—a travel commercial for Seattle," Mari said, and looked at me. "The dancing in the rain is perfect, but it was so unique it didn't seem to fit in with some of your other scenes, you know?"

"I wanted more Z flair," Mari said. "We barely saw you except for the shot on your porch."

"Yeah!" Lauren seconded. "Your vlogs are so great because it's all you."

I nodded, jotting down notes, and trying to hide that I was blinking back tears. I didn't want my friends to think I didn't appreciate them sharing their thoughts, but it was hard to hear them say they didn't love the film I had been working so hard on. "Okay," I said quietly. "Thanks for being honest."

"You'll get there, Z," Lauren said. "Maybe you just need to rearrange things."

"Or maybe you just need to simplify," Becka suggested.

"Whatever the fix is, we know you can do it," Mari said. "The great Z never fails!"

"Thanks." I tried to smile, but I was feeling pretty crummy. My movie wasn't working. I'd concentrated so much on how it looked rather than the story I was trying to tell. But now I had only four weeks to make it right. I was pretty nervous I wouldn't get it done in time. But there was only one way to find out.

"Thanks, guys," I said. "I guess I better get back to work."

Chapter 10

What's Your Story?

Ticktock. Ticktock.

I could feel the minutes slipping away with each passing day. I dreamed of clocks and calendars and never finishing my movie. I still hadn't figured out my story.

During the next several days, I re-watched my movie over and over again. I pulled scenes apart in separate windows and tried to figure out which parts were working and which weren't. I had two columns. On the left were the scenes that I felt worked: Mari's band in the rain, me on my front porch, walking through the neighborhood with Popcorn, and the footage at the Beanery and Sweet Treats. On the right were all my interviews and pretty generic shots of Seattle. Becka was right: The landmark footage and the drone shots of the Locks felt like they belonged in a different movie. If I ever shot a tourist film of Seattle, I'd break them back out, but for this film, they were gone. That meant I was losing almost three minutes of my ten-minute movie. *Gulp.*

Mom popped in one afternoon while I was working on my laptop. "How's the editing coming?" she asked, carrying in a glass of iced tea and some cookies on a plate. Popcorn picked her head up from my bed when she saw the food.

"Not great," I admitted, and spun around in my computer chair to face her. "Mom?" I hesitated. "Have you ever made a movie and realized too late that your movie doesn't have a story to tell?"

"Hmm . . . that's a big problem," Mom said, sitting down on my bed by Popcorn. "But I've had it happen." I looked at her in surprise. "It's easy to lose your way on a project. You get so caught up in the details sometimes your story gets lost in the shuffle."

"That sounds familiar," I told her. "I was so worried about making this movie *the best ever* that now it looks like someone else's film. My hands made it, my brain made it, but I'm not sure my heart's in it. It's not *me*."

Mom laughed and walked over to me. "So what happened?"

"I don't know." I shrugged. "I guess I got so carried away listening to what everyone else thought I should include that I forgot what I wanted my movie to say in the first place. And it's like we talked about in the archive. I kept trying to act like I knew what I was doing but didn't stop to really figure it out." I looked at Mom. "Now I don't know how to fix this."

"Want to show me what you have already and we can try to figure out the problem?" Mom asked.

I nodded. I pulled up my movie and pressed PLAY. Mom watched quietly and then at the end she looked at me. "I'm going to ask you the same question I ask my students: What is this movie trying to show the viewer?"

I was stumped. "I don't know," I said. "I wanted it to show things about me and my life here, but I think I forgot to include enough me in my story." Mom nodded, encouraging me to go on. "It's, like, I have a lot of cool pieces—like, my friends and my time with Popcorn and stuff, but then I added in all these other things that keep my story from fitting together."

Mom nodded again. "I see that." She squeezed my

hand. "I think you're making progress here. Finding your story can be the hardest part of filmmaking." She smiled. "I have no doubt you can find yours."

What was my Seattle story? I wondered. I looked at my footage, listed out in the two columns. I wasn't exactly sure yet, but I had a feeling I was getting closer to figuring it out. I needed to take a risk now with this movie. I didn't want this to be a movie about any old person's experience of Seattle. I wanted it to be about my Seattle.

My Seattle.

Z's Seattle.

Zeattle?

I thought about the idea more and more. In between classes, during breakfast, while watching TV, I wrote lists about what I loved about my life in Seattle. I knew if I wrote down all the things that made my city my own, I'd figure out what I'd been missing.

"Would you guys want to watch a short film about one person's real life in Seattle?" I asked Becka and Gigi when I video chatted with them that afternoon. Mari and Lauren were over so we could work on posters for Lauren's soccer tournament that coming weekend. "Something that showed you what a person was like, who their friends were, what their family was like, and how they had the most amazing dog in the world?" Popcorn barked as if on cue.

Becka and Gigi laughed.

"Now that sounds like a movie I want to see!" Becka said. "What are you thinking?"

Lauren and Mari had walked closer to my computer to hear more. "I'm thinking of calling it 'Zeattle'. Get it? Z's Seattle? And it would be a typical day in the life. Something that would make you feel like you know me, even if you don't."

"Nice!" Mari marveled.

"Right? And it would have to be really authentic—the real Z." I went on, cautiously, "Like, how the real me worries that I don't know what I'm doing all the time."

"Is that true?" Mari frowned. "You always act like you know what you're doing."

I shook my head. "I don't! I try to be upbeat, but sometimes I wonder if the ideas I have are good enough."

"Z, your ideas are gold!" Lauren scolded me. "You should have told us you were stressing out."

"I know, but I wanted you guys to think I knew what I was doing. I love vlogging and making AGSMs, and I try to be the best I can be for the Z. Crew, but sometimes I sort of drown in the pressure," I told them. "I think I got so caught up in trying to win CloudSong that I forgot what I liked about making films in the first place."

"At least you're trying!" Lauren said. "I wish I could admit when I needed some help. On the field, no one can get in my way, no matter if I'm doing an outside of the foot pass, a double scissors move and a chip shot, or whatever, but give me a timed test and I break out in a cold sweat. I never tell anyone that."

"Same here," Becka said quietly. "I hardly ever tell people that being in this wheelchair and doing physical therapy is exhausting. Sometimes I just want to hide away from the world in my room."

"I didn't know that," I said in surprise. "You're always so happy!"

"We travel so much, it's hard to make friends," Gigi blurted out. "I know everyone thinks it's so cool that I go to all these places, and it is, but I hate that whenever

I find someone to hang out with, we're ready to move on to a new city. Then I have to start all over again. It gets lonely."

"Why didn't you tell us that?" Becka asked.

Gigi shrugged. "I guess I was afraid for people to see the real me and judge me for it."

"I'm like that sometimes, too," Mari added. "I know I call myself the Queen of Fashion, but I worry about how I look a lot."

"You?" I sputtered. I couldn't believe what I'm hearing. "But you always look amazing!"

"But I don't always *feel* amazing," Mari said.

"Why haven't we been telling each other these things?" Lauren asked, sounding almost annoyed with herself and the rest of us.

"Yeah!" I added, getting fired up, too. "We're friends! If something is bothering us, we should speak up. Be real. Like we are right now."

"We should definitely do this more often," Mari agreed. "Maybe if we all stopped getting so caught up in taking sixty selfies before we post one or reshooting the same video twenty times till it looks flawless, we'd be better off. Life isn't perfect. Why should we pretend that it is online?"

"So let's stop pretending," I said, feeling inspired. I jumped up and grabbed my phone and Popcorn wandered over to see what the fuss was about. I held my phone to my chest shyly. "Would you guys want to be part of my vlog this week? We could take turns telling *our* stories—which are the best kind of stories there are."

"I'd like that," Lauren said, nodding.

"Me, too," Mari said, and stood up excitedly.

"I'm in!" Gigi said.

"Me, three!" shouted Becka. "Hey! Maybe we should use a hashtag so others in the Z. Crew could tell their story, too."

I grinned. "What about something like 'the real me'? Then others could post their stories, and we'd be able to find theirs, too."

"Let's start right now!" Mari suggested. "Gigi and Becka can film their stories, then we can add them to ours and try to put a post up this week."

"Sounds like a plan to me!" I turned my camera on Popcorn and pressed RECORD. "You first, Popcorn. What's your story? Do you secretly like cats?" Popcorn actually growled, and we all laughed.

As I looked around my room, I knew this was a

What's Your Story?

Zeattle moment, the kind I was going to fill my movie with. And if CloudSong didn't like what they saw, that would be okay. I was going to make a film that told my story—a story about having fun and getting inspired, and filled with the best kind of friends.

Chapter 11

The Real Me

For the next week and a half, I filmed and edited my new, improved, and oh-so-fabulously-Z movie. It felt different the minute I started putting it together. For the first time during this whole CloudSong contest, I was enjoying myself. It was just me and my world through my lens. The parts I kept and the new parts I added in fit together like puzzle pieces.

On the day of the deadline, I was ready to submit my movie. If the judges liked it, great, and if they didn't, I was still Z, an aspiring filmmaker who would make it big some day! *CloudSong Film Festival*, I thought, *I'm coming for you!*

"Mom said she'll be home in ten minutes," Dad said as Lauren, Mari, and I had an afterschool snack in my kitchen. "Then we'll get down to business!"

My friends had come over after school to help me

press SEND on my CloudSong e-mail. I wanted Mom to be there, too. I knew this cut of the film was my best, but I still felt some butterflies fluttering madly in my stomach when I thought about sending my movie off to be judged. It was exciting and a little bit scary at the same time. I needed a distraction.

"Let's see if there are any new comments on the video about 'The Real Me,'" I said. Mom and Dad had loved the video post I had done with my friends, and we had put it up a few days earlier.

"Sure," Dad said, and I ran upstairs to get my laptop. Dad had cleared off the kitchen island by the time I got back, and I opened the video post and looked for new comments using our hashtag. Dad, Lauren, and Mari huddled around the laptop, too.

"Hey, look, there's Maddie's," Lauren pointed out. We clicked on Maddie's video.

"Sometimes I get quiet when I'm in a large group," Maddie said. "People think I'm not interested in what they have to say or think that I'm being rude, but the truth is, large crowds make me nervous. I like talking to friends one-on-one."

Andrew jumped into the frame and put an arm

around her. "That's what I'm here for!" We all laughed. So did Maddie on-screen.

"What about you?" she asked, her brown eyes shining like they always did when she was reporting for Camera Club. "Tell us about the real you."

Andrew looked panicked for a moment, like a camera flash went off in his face. "Me . . . uh . . ."

"What's something I—or we—don't know about you?" Maddie pressed him.

Andrew sighed. "Okay. Confession time: I'm in a hip-hop dance class."

"What?" Maddie questioned from on-screen. Dad, Lauren, Mari, and I said the same thing out loud, too.

Andrew nodded. "It's true. I've been dancing for the last five years. I love it, but I never talk about it because I don't know what people are going to think."

"*Think?*" Maddie asked. "That's so cool! Show me some moves right now."

"No way!" Andrew protested. Then he looked at the camera. "Maybe next time. When I have music, and Z is there to make sure I'm filmed in the perfect lighting."

I cracked up. I would have to text Andrew later and tell him I was in. He was getting a hip-hop video! I was learning so much about the Z. Crew and my friends with this hashtag. I went back to the original video. There were more than four hundred fifty comments!

Lauren leaned over my shoulder. "Wow! One hundred and sixty new comments today?! I still can't believe you finished editing your movie *and* got this video post done this week."

"Look at some of these comments," Dad said, looking at the screen. "'The real me likes playing video games more than I like dolls.' And this one: 'The real me hates playing sports, but I love my still-life art class I just started taking.'"

"Can we comment back on all of these?" Lauren asked.

"Dad and I have been trying to, but there are so many." I stared at the growing list in awe.

"Let's do a few now," Dad said.

"I'll pick one!" Mari pointed to the screen. "Hey, there's one about fashion." She dictated her reply as she typed it. "Fashion is about finding your own style and being comfortable in your own skin. Wear what you love and be proud!" Dad nodded, and she hit SEND. "This is fun!"

The *Real* **Z**

Popcorn jumped up and her paws accidentally hit the keyboard. Our video started to play. "Oh, Popcorn," I said and went to stop the video.

"Wait!" Lauren said. "I want to watch it again. I think it's your best post ever."

I gave in. We all watched as my face came on the screen.

"Hi, Z. Crew!" I heard myself say. "If we're all going to be part of the same 'crew,' then I thought we should get to know each other a little better. So today we're being real and sharing things about ourselves that make us unique. Don't be shy! I'll even go first." I launched into how worried I've been about my film and how sometimes I panic that I'll never be as good of a filmmaker as I want to be. Then the shot cut to Lauren and Mari, and they took turns telling their stories, with me adding in photos I had of Lauren on the soccer field and Mari playing with her band. I spliced Gigi's and Becka's videos into our post, too, with travel pics from Gigi and video of Becka kicking butt at wheelchair basketball. Then I came back on to wrap things up.

"So what do you say, Z. Crew?" I asked. "Do you want to share your story? Comment, post your own video, or tweet with the hashtag 'the real me' and let's get real. That's what friends are for—to help us through the hard times and be there with us when it's time to laugh, too. When we come together as a crew, we are stronger than we could ever be alone." I smiled and Lauren and Mari appeared in the shot, too. "Z. Crew out!"

Mom walked into the kitchen carrying a bag of groceries. "Were you watching the video post again?" I nodded. "I showed it to some other professors today and we all agreed—you are a true filmmaker."

"Mom!" I blushed. "Stop."

She wrapped her arms around me. "I'm serious! We're so proud of you. No matter what happens with CloudSong, that video you made proves you know what you're doing. This is what real artists do—they spark conversations and create movements—and you've done that with this post."

"Maybe we should do a follow-up video on how inspired we are by everyone's posts and encourage people to keep them coming?" I suggested, and Lauren and Mari nodded enthusiastically.

"Great idea, but don't you have something to do first?" Dad asked, nodding to the computer.

The *Real* Z

"Yes! I guess it's time." I closed the video window and opened my inbox. I'd already composed my submission e-mail earlier. "Okay, this is it." I wiggled my fingers and breathed in and out.

"You got this, Z!" Lauren shouted.

"Power to the Z. Crew!" Mari chanted.

"This is your moment," Mom said, sounding excited.

"No matter what happens, we are so proud of you," Dad added.

I was ready.

Everyone leaned around the kitchen island to watch. Here . . . we . . . go. I closed my eyes and pressed SEND.

Woo-hoo! My movie was officially submitted!

"I did it! I just officially entered a movie in my first film festival!" Everyone applauded.

"Does this mean we can see the movie now?" Lauren begged.

"Please?" Mari seconded.

I looked at Mom. We came up with this idea together. "Not yet," I said. My friends groaned. "I want us all to see it together when it makes it into the festival."

"I love how you just said *when* it makes it into the festival," Mari said.

"We should celebrate," Dad suggested. "You can pick what we have for dinner tonight."

Oooh. I liked the sound of that. There were so many choices. Baked ziti? Bossam, my favorite Korean dish? Or did I go with my old standby—a good burger and fries? I was torn.

Ping!

I glanced at the laptop. "CloudSong already sent a reply!" I said, surprised.

"What does it say?" Dad asked.

I opened the e-mail and saw the small paragraph. My heart sunk ever so slightly. There was a tiny part of me that hoped someone had opened my movie up right away, watched it, and thought it was too brilliant to wait any longer to tell me.

> Thank you for your CloudSong entry. We look forward to viewing your submission! A final decision will be made by May 15. In the meantime, we ask you to be a judge as well. As future filmmakers, we would love for you to vote on your fellow young filmmaker grant entries. Visit the CloudSong website to watch them and weigh in. Happy viewing!

The *Real* Z

"Wow, we can see the other submissions?" I said aloud and quickly clicked on the link. "I want to see what other people did!"

"None of them are going to be as good as yours," Lauren said like the true bestie she was.

I snorted. "I'm not so sure about that," I said as the first film loaded.

We gathered around as the video began to play. I wasn't sure what I was watching at first because it was really dark. Then things slowly came into focus.

"Where is he, a basement?" Mari asked.

"No, I think he's in the Seattle underground," I said.

A boy around my age, maybe slightly older, had done his whole film about the tunnels and secret passageways below the streets of the city. The passageways used to be at street level in the middle of the nineteenth century, but then the streets were elevated and the passages became abandoned. Now people could take tours of the underground. The boy climbed up and down ladders, and through tunnels to show us all these hidden doorways and rooms and even how the tunnels held up when there were heavy rains. It was actually really cool.

The next movie was done by a girl who said she

loved anything "creepy cool" in Seattle. Her movie was about visiting all her favorite "haunts" like an odd shop that supposedly sold haunted artifacts, and a tour of the cemetery to see the tombstones of martial arts actors Bruce and Brandon Lee. There were less spooky stops on her tour, too, like a visit to a giant shoe museum!

"That one was bizarre," Mari said.

"But really unique," I said. I was in awe of how they'd both come up with pieces of Seattle culture that I'd never even thought about before. Both movies were so different, yet interesting. "I never would have thought to do something like either of those."

"That's because Seattle underground and haunted tours of cemeteries aren't your thing," Lauren said.

"Lauren is right," Mom added. "Their films reflect what they like about their hometown. Your film reflects you."

My stomach still felt a little jittery. Those submissions were going to be tough competition. And they weren't the only ones I was going up against. I tried to push any doubts out of my mind. I couldn't change things now. Honestly, I wouldn't even if I could.

"You're right," I said. I closed the submission window. Mom, Dad, and I could watch more films later. "I told my story. I can't do better than that, can I?"

"Not at all," Mom agreed.

I smiled at her. No matter how this contest ended, I'd given it my best shot.

Chapter 12

"The Horrible Homework Hacker"

"No! It can't be!" Lauren shouted from off camera in her best character-in-peril voice. "The Horrible Homework Hacker has struck again!"

We'd cast two of our usual American Girl dolls to star in the movie based on Lauren's excellent script about friends whose homework keeps mysteriously disappearing when they leave their desks. Lauren had taken on the dual role of screenwriter and prop master, making a laptop out of a book wrapped in aluminum foil and a keyboard out of poster board. Mari had come over to style the dolls' outfits—they looked great in jeans and tees, and we gave one doll a beret. My lights and backdrop were set up on the floor of my room. Even Popcorn was behaving.

The dolls were performing beautifully.

It was two weeks after I submitted my CloudSong entry, and I was way too busy to even wonder when that long-awaited little e-mail about finalists was going to show up in my inbox.

I wasn't thinking about that e-mail at all.

Not a bit.

Okay, maybe a little bit.

Still, filming "The Horrible Homework Hacker" was a good distraction!

Lauren and Mari had already recorded the dolls' voice-overs, and now we were shooting the video in stop-motion. Lauren played the next line back again.

"Mr. Kozak is never going to believe our homework was stolen three times!" Lauren said. "We have to catch this hacker in the act and set a trap."

Mari's voice came next. "Let's leave another sheet of homework and a flash drive out and see if the Hacker comes back to get it."

Lauren pressed PAUSE on the recording.

We reviewed our storyboard before setting up the next shot with the dolls. We'd chosen this huge, oversize teddy bear Lauren won at a carnival basketball game to be the actual Hacker, but it was so big, we were having trouble establishing the shot.

"Want to let the voice-over continue to play as we figure this out?" Lauren asked. "Maybe it will give us ideas."

"Good idea," I agreed, and Mari nodded.

"Let's go get something to eat and leave our homework *right here*," Mari said dramatically on the voice over. "I hope the Homework Hacker doesn't come steal it!"

"He won't!" Lauren's character said. "We'll be gone only a minute."

"Mwah-hah-hah!" I heard myself say in my best spooky voice, acting as the hacker. "Homework! I must eat more homework!"

"He's falling for it," we heard Lauren fake whisper. The three of us stared at the setup, concentrating hard.

Suddenly, Popcorn burst onto the set, knocking down the dolls and the small desk! She'd gotten herself wrapped up in Mari's knit wrap and couldn't shake the jacket off. The three of us started laughing.

"Duh-duh-duh! We've found our Homework Hacker! It's Popcorn!" I said jokingly.

Lauren stopped laughing. "Hey! That's not bad! How can we convince Popcorn to come into the shot? Maybe she can be the Homework Hacker instead of a stuffed animal."

Before we could figure out how to make that idea work, I heard chords from Needles in a Haystack's version of "Singin' in the Rain" begin to play. Mari had sent me a clip to use as my e-mail alert.

I glanced at the e-mail notification.

"CloudSong," I said, trying not to freak out. "I can't look." I covered my eyes. I momentarily pictured the subject line saying "Thanks for entering, but better luck next year."

I heard Lauren and Mari's voices. "Open it!"

My heart started to thump faster. I pulled my purple beanie cap over my eyes. *Either way, I did my best,* I reminded myself, thinking of what Dad and Mom would say. I held my breath. "Maybe one of you should read it."

"Okay. This is the subject line." Mari began to read: "CloudSong Seattle Film Festival Young Filmmakers' Contest Update."

"Wait!" I burst out.

What if this was the moment that launched my whole filmmaking career? Did I really want to be in a documentary about my life someday and have to admit I was too freaked out to open my first film festival results e-mail?

"I'll read it," I said. I pulled the cap away from my eyes and, without hesitating, stared at the e-mail. It was pretty long, but I scanned it quickly. I had won second prize and that meant my movie was going to be shown at the festival in a few weeks!

Oh. My. Awesomesauce!

"I'm in!" I shouted.

The three of us started to scream, and then Popcorn began to bark. Mom and Dad came running up the stairs and into my room.

"Everything okay?" Dad asked. When he saw us jumping up and down, he grinned. "Is it CloudSong?"

"What did they say?" Mom asked anxiously.

"I came in second place!" I said happily. Both Mom and Dad hugged me.

"It's a bummer about the prize money," Mari said quietly.

"Yeah, but to be honest, I'm too excited to worry

about it," I said. We'd have to think of something else to do at Camera Club until we got a new camera. Some kids were shooting videos on their phones. Others brought in their family's camera. No matter what, I knew there was no way we'd stop making videos. "That one by the kid who focused on the Seattle underground came in first. His was really good."

"Second place is still amazing," Lauren said firmly.

"And you're still number one in my book," Dad said.

"You have to tell Becka and Gigi," Mari reminded me.

"I'll text them to log on for a chat," Lauren said, and her fingers flew across her screen. Seconds later, I heard the pings for their replies. Mari opened up the chat screen on my computer.

"Did you hear from the festival?" Gigi asked. "What did they say?"

"Do we need to beg our parents to let us fly in for a premiere?" Becka asked.

"Yes! I came in second," I said proudly. "My movie is going to be shown at the festival."

"Aces, Z!" Gigi shouted as Becka chanted, *"Team Z! Team Z!"*

I was so happy, I felt like I could burst. "I can't believe it!" I said again. "I really can't believe it!"

"We can." Mom smiled. "I know you struggled trying to find your story, but look what happened once you did—everything came together."

"I already know what your next film topic should be," Dad added. "A movie about the coolest dad on the planet."

We all laughed. "Definitely," I said. "I'll get right on it."

I knew in my heart that there would be a next time and a next time after that. I had a million stories to tell—I couldn't wait to start sharing them.

CHAPTER 13

My Big Night

"**W**ho do we have pulling up in a limo? Is that Z Yang, the most buzzed-about young filmmaker on the planet? Why it is! The crowd is going wild for her, ladies and gentlemen!" Dad held up his fist and talked into it like a microphone. "We have heard a lot about her groundbreaking documentary *Zeattle* this week, and it sounds like these fans can't wait to see more from the first-time filmmaker. What is the crowd saying? 'Z! Z! Z!' "

"Dad!" I groaned, but I secretly loved it.

How could I not?

I'd dreamed about attending my own film premiere forever and now it was no longer a dream—it was actually happening!

The five of us—Mom, Dad, Lauren, Mari, and I— were in my family's Jeep and headed to the downtown theater hosting the festival. I knew there wouldn't be a crowd waiting. Even if there was one, they weren't going to be looking for me. No one knew who I was . . .

Yet.

Mari was getting into the same spirit Dad was. She leaned over to me, pretending her fist was a microphone. "Z, can you tell us who your stylist is? That outfit you're rocking is outrageous!" Mari's was great, too. She had on a tie-dye *Team Z* T-shirt that she'd paired with a white-washed denim skirt, and had accessorized with a big, beaded necklace. Her curls were piled high on her head, and she had a funky yellow butterfly clip in her hair.

I grabbed Mari's "microphone." "Thank you. I can't take credit for my outfit. The look was put together by my good friend Mariela Ramirez." I looked down at my black embroidered skirt that Mari had suggested I wear with a purple shimmery tank top and a long, dangling silver necklace. "You'll be able to find her own line of clothes in stores nationwide this fall along with her band's first full-length album."

Mari stole her hand back and smiled. "Now you're pushing it!"

"No, she's not," Lauren said as she brushed a piece of string off her skirt. "Z won a film festival. Why can't you start your own clothing line and work on an album while I get invited to play on a professional soccer team?"

"I love what I'm hearing, girls," Mom said. "Dream big."

"We already are," I said as I looked out the window at Seattle's streets.

I was on my way to my first festival, where my movie—*my movie!*—was going to premiere before a full-length film! I didn't think what Mari, Lauren, and I were fantasizing about was so far out of reach anymore.

My phone buzzed. I pulled it out of the small black clutch Mari had lent me.

> **GIGI:** Sending you good vibes! Have a great time at the film premiere! Can't wait to hear about it!
>
> **BECKA:** Seattle is going to love Zeattle! I can feel it!

My friends were the best. I knew no matter what the audience thought of my movie at the screening, the people who were important to me were really proud. And I was, too.

After parking the car, we headed to the theater.

"Are you ready for this?" Mom asked as we walked, arms linked.

"Yeah!" I said, then hesitated. "Also nervous, excited, freaked out, and totally pumped up. I want to remember every moment of this night forever."

"You will," Mom said. "This is a big night! You'll always look back on it proudly. So will I. You're really coming into your own, Z."

Mom was making me misty-eyed. "I really hope you like the movie."

"Of course we will," Dad said. "You put your all into this."

We rounded the corner to the front of the theater, and I saw it right away. There *was* a red carpet! And photographers! There were even people being interviewed by a camera crew! (Sadly, there were no crowds waiting on the street corner with "Z" signs. Next time.) We walked up to a woman with a clipboard who was standing outside the roped-off area. When she saw us, she looked down at her clipboard again and smiled.

"Hi! Are you Suzanne Yang and family?" she asked.

"Yes," I said, "but you can call me Z. How'd you know it was me?"

She turned the clipboard around and I saw my school photo. I forgot I'd submitted one with the application. "You look just like your picture." She let us into a roped-off area. "Your party has seats reserved in theater one."

That was so cool! I felt like a star.

"Thank you," I said. "I guess we should get seated."

"Actually, before you go in, we were hoping you would talk to a reporter from the *Seattle Tribune*," said the woman. "She's here to do a piece on the young filmmakers in the festival. She's waiting on the carpet with a photographer. Do you mind talking to the press?"

"Mind? I'd love it!" I said. Mari and Lauren squealed—quietly. We were trying to be chill, but this was surreal! I was about to be interviewed on a red carpet!

"Great, I'll bring you over," the woman said.

"Do you mind if my family and friends come along?" I asked.

"Of course not. They can stand right by you on the carpet." She led the way.

Wow! Lauren mouthed.

We weaved through a small crowd onto the red

carpet where things were much louder. Reporters were asking other guests questions and photographers were snapping away. The woman introduced me to the reporter, Katy.

"Hi, Z! Congratulations on receiving one of CloudSong's prestigious young filmmaker awards," said Katy. "What do you think it was about your entry that made you stand out?" She held a microphone out to me.

I tried to calm down and focus on the answer. I'd never been interviewed before. "Hopefully, they noticed how I tried to stay true to myself," I said. "When I first started working on my film, I got a little lost, but then I thought about the movie I really wanted to make, and the story I wanted to tell, and it all came together. I realized I wanted to share a piece of Seattle that was entirely my own. That's what I tried to do in *Zeattle*."

"Sounds like it worked!" Katy said, holding the mic steady. She asked me a few more questions about my age, where I went to school, and who my favorite director was. (I refused to play favorites, instead listing a bunch.) "I hope you have fun at your premiere tonight," she said, wrapping up.

"I will . . . I mean *we* will," I corrected myself. I called everyone over. "My parents and my friends came with me tonight." Lauren looked nervous, but Mari held her arm. "I couldn't have made this movie without them."

"We should get a picture of you together," Katy suggested. She motioned to her photographer. The five of us posed with our arms around each other. Mari linked one of her arms with mine, and I linked my free arm with Lauren's. Mom and Dad were the book ends.

"Smile!" the photographer said. There were a series of flashes and clicks. "Now one of the winner alone." Everyone else stepped back, and I didn't know if I should pose or twirl or smile or do all three. I just stood there all bashful and awkward instead. I should have had Mari practice paparazzi skills with me. Next time!

Everything after that happened so fast. We walked into the theater and were offered free sodas and popcorn. Then an usher showed us to our seats, which had little signs on them with my name! As we slid into the row, I noticed the theater was packed. I settled into my seat between Mom and Lauren and tried not to fidget as I stared at the blank screen.

Any minute, the lights would go down and I would be watching my movie.

In a theater.

With an audience.

I felt like I was on a roller coaster that was going up, up, up, and I knew any second we'd go whooshing down. Everyone around us was talking and laughing, but I kept my eyes on the screen and waited for it to flicker to life. When the lights finally began to dim, Mom squeezed my hand. I squeezed back.

"I'm so excited!" Lauren whispered in my ear.

Mari leaned over Lauren. "We finally get to see your movie! It's going to be great!"

The room darkened, and I saw the title credits and my name.

"Zeattle"

A Film by Z Yang

And then the movie started.

The film opened with the drone footage of my neighborhood, flying over my block and landing on my front porch, where I stood waiting. "Hi, I'm Z Yang!" I said. "And this is my home in Seattle, Washington. I could tell you why I love living in this city, but I thought it would be more fun if I showed you. So come along on

a typical Z kind of day!" I motioned to the viewer to follow me as I splashed around in puddles with Popcorn
and gave them a front row seat on my scooter as
Mari and I zoomed to school.

"You're making me dizzy!" Dad teased in a
whisper.

I made a montage of a Camera Club meeting and then Lauren and I walked the viewers along
our favorite street in Queen Anne and took them to
Sweet Treats, where Andrew and Maddie were
waiting with bags of candy. "I don't come here every
day," I said into the camera, "but I suffered for the
sake of art."

That got some laughs! Lauren and I scootered home
as it began to drizzle, which was perfect because it tran-
sitioned into my favorite part of the film: Mari's band
dancing in the rain.

"You know the best part about my life in Seattle?" I
asked as I stood and twirled an umbrella on my block
and then walked to the park where we tried to shoot
the music video. "I love when I get to go 'Singin' in the
Rain.'" Then I cut to the footage of Needles in a Haystack
dancing, with their version of "Singin' in the Rain"

playing in the background. To make the scene more personal, I had even added the footage Mom took of me joining in.

After some shots of dinner at my house (we had bulgogi, and I talked about some of our other favorite Korean traditions), it was time to go to my room and show my filmmaking studio where I make all my AGSM videos. "It's been nice having you along with me today," I said from my computer chair. I pretended to yawn. "But it's been a long day, and it is time for me to turn in. Good night, Seattle!"

My film cut to black and the credits started to roll. I waited to see if I'd hear a magic sound . . .

There it was! Applause!

The audience was clapping for me! And they were clapping loudly!

I looked at my parents and friends in astonishment. They all stood up and gave me a standing ovation! Dad was filming with his phone, and Mom was taking pictures. Her eyes looked teary.

Lauren yelled to me over the applause. "Stand up, Z! Let everyone see you!"

So I rose. I looked around at my family and my

friends, and smiled bigger, stood taller, and soaked it all in. Mom was right. I was never going to forget this moment.

"Come on, Z! Take a bow!" Mari cheered.

I blushed, but my friends and parents clapped even louder and I couldn't help but smile. It had been a bumpy road, but I'd done it—I'd made a movie I was proud of, and it premiered at a film festival!

Chapter 14

A Fresh Start

I was sitting in Ms. Garner's class paying excellent attention to the math equation on the board (I'd learned my lesson there!) when there was an announcement over the loud speaker.

"Attention all members of Camera Club," I heard Mr. Mullolly say. "Emergency meeting during free period today. Please be there. Thank you."

I glanced at Lauren, who shrugged.

Emergency meeting? That didn't sound good.

Was it about our broken camera? Mr. Mullolly had lent us his tablet for the last few weeks to work on our assignments, but we still didn't have a real camera for the club. Without my prize money, I didn't see us getting a camera anytime soon. I was still a little sad that I hadn't saved the day, but I knew I had tried my best.

"We'll figure out a way to keep reporting," Lauren had said.

I hoped she was right, but I was worried. Other clubs had shut down before. What if Camera Club was on its way out?

After class, Lauren and I headed to the media room off the library. We were a little slow, since Lauren kept stopping to ask me things about the math class we'd just had, and point things out in her book. The bell rang.

"Lauren," I wailed. "We're already late!"

"Sorry!" she said, and sped up.

"Can you open the door?" Lauren asked when we arrived. Her arms were full of books.

"Sure," I said, and turned the knob.

"Congratulations, Z!" everyone shouted as we walked through the door, startling me.

"What . . . wow!" I said, trying to find the words.

The entire Camera Club was there, with balloons and a huge CONGRATULATIONS banner hanging from one wall. On the table were colorful napkins, plates, and pink and purple cupcakes with tiny director clapboards on them.

"We wanted you to know how proud we are that one of Camera Club's reporters had a film shown in the

CloudSong Film Festival," Mr. Mullolly said. "I hope you'll share it with us one day during a meeting so we can all watch it."

"Thank you!" I said to everyone, blushing. "It's so nice of all you guys to do this."

"Why doesn't everyone grab a cupcake, and we'll go over some club business while we're here," Mr. Mullolly suggested.

I took a seat with Maddie, Andrew, and Lauren.

"You sneak," I said to Lauren. "You didn't really need to ask me math questions!"

Lauren laughed. "I had to stall you somehow."

"So our first order of business is still how we manage to keep producing a news segment for Pine Crest Middle School without having a camera," Mr. Mullolly said.

I looked at Lauren worriedly. I could picture Mr. Mullolly telling us we had to end the club for the year. I didn't want that to happen! "I don't mind lending you all my tablet when I can, but sometimes I need it myself, so I wanted to see if we could brainstorm other ways we can keep working while we petition the school for funds to buy a new one. Any suggestions?"

Everyone started murmuring, and I wracked my

brain for an answer. I'd been as worried as everyone else about what would happen to our club, but I realized now I didn't need to be. We just had to think outside the box, just like I had to do when I didn't love my first film edit.

The Camera Club had a story to tell. Lots of stories! And we didn't need a pricey camera to do it. I smiled to myself. If we were creative, we could come up with tons of ways to tell our school's stories together.

I raised my hand.

"Z?" Mr. Mullolly called on me.

"Well, I know filming on a real camera is best, but I'm re-thinking the idea of using our phones and web-cams. Sometimes I use both of those for my blog," I explained to the group. "I even used some phone foot-age for my CloudSong movie. There are some great apps for video editing and taping that I'd be happy to share with everyone. We can probably do segments that look as good—if not better—than what we've done before."

"That's what I'm talking about," Mr. Mullolly said enthusiastically. "Storytelling can be done in different ways. Thanks, Z! Andrew?"

"Well, this isn't about filming, per se, but I was thinking maybe we could post our news segment to the school website so that students who miss the broadcast the first time can watch it later," Andrew suggested.

"Or their parents can watch their kids if they're featured in a segment," Maddie added.

Slowly, others started to raise their hands, too, and gave some great suggestions for ways to film and for how to get our videos out there.

I looked at my friends. Lauren, Maddie, Andrew, and I were all smiling. Mr. M was grinning, too. "These ideas are great. Can someone start a list?"

"I will!" Maddie volunteered, ripping a page out of one of her notebooks. She started taking notes.

I watched as Maddie's list got so long she needed a second page. One idea would spark another, and another, and we couldn't stop! All it took was one bit of inspiration. A vision, as Mom would call it.

It made me wonder what my next film was going to be. And I knew there *would* be a next film. I couldn't wait to dig into a new project.

But not quite yet.

First, I had some major celebrating to do.

Z. Crew out!

About the *Author*

Jen Calonita graduated from Boston College where she majored in communications. This degree helped her land a job at a teen magazine where she got to interview several of her favorite movie and music stars! These days, Jen writes books for young readers, including the Fairy Tale Reform School series. She also has written the Secrets of My Hollywood Life series for teens. *The Real Z* is her nineteenth novel. When she isn't working, Jen loves going running, taking pictures, and hanging out with her husband and two boys at their home on Long Island in New York. She also enjoys going on walks with her feisty Chihuahua named Jack, where just like Z, Jen does her best brainstorming for whatever project she's working on next.

Ready
to join
the  **Z.**

Crew?

Visit
americangirl.com to check out Z's vlog!

⏮ ⏸ ▶ ⏭

MEET

TENNEY GRANT!

Her **biggest** dream is to
*share what's in her
heart through music.*

Turn the page to read an excerpt from
Tenney's first book!

LOST IN THE MUSIC

Chapter 1

*M*y left hand shifted down the neck of my guitar, fingers pressing into the frets to form chords, while my right hand sailed over the strings with my favorite pick. I knew every note of "April Springs." I didn't have to look at my sheet music or think about how to play the song. I just let go and played, feeling the music as if it was flowing out of my heart.

Out of the corner of my eye, I caught Dad waving me down from a few feet away.

Startled, I clamped my hand over my guitar's neck, muting its sound mid-chord. It took me a moment to realize I didn't hear the buzzy twang of Dad's bass guitar. I glanced around. The rest of our band wasn't playing, either.

"Sorry," I said, feeling my cheeks turn hot pink.

★ ★

LOST IN THE MUSIC

"No worries," Dad said, winking. "I know you love that one. And you were singing with so much heart that it nearly broke mine to stop you."

I blushed. When I play a song I love, it's easy for me to get swept up and forget about everything but the music. "April Springs" has a slow, sad melody that fills me with warmth every time we rehearse it. And when I sing its romantic lyrics, I can't help daydreaming about what the songwriter must have been feeling when she composed them.

"That transition out of the chorus still sounds a bit rocky," Dad said to the band. "Let's try it again."

Our lead singer, Jesse, wrinkled her nose at him. "Come on, Ray. This is the fifth time we've gone over the chorus. Let's just move on to the next song."

My seventeen-year-old brother, Mason, rolled his eyes from behind his drum kit. Mason isn't Jesse's biggest fan. He thinks she's stuck-up because she never helps unpack gear at our shows. Also, she only drinks bottled water from France, even though the tap water is perfectly fine here in Nashville, Tennessee. Despite all that, I couldn't help but admire her. Jesse definitely had what it took to be a lead singer for a band. She had a great voice, she loved performing, and she was happiest when she was the center of attention. Every time I watched her perform I wondered: *Could that be me someday?*

"Let's try the chorus *once* more," Dad replied calmly. "We haven't practiced in ages. And with our next show around the corner, I want to make sure we have this down."

Jesse pouted, but she knew she couldn't say no because the Tri-Stars were Dad's band.

The Tri-Stars used to be a family band. But when Mom quit to start her own food truck business, Dad invited Jesse to join us as the lead singer. I wish we got to perform at the big stages around Nashville, like the Ryman Auditorium or the Grand Ole Opry, but we mostly just play weekend gigs around our neighborhood. Even so, we have a few fans—that is, if you count my little sister and my best friend.

Jesse sighed. "Let's get on with it, then." She counted off, and the four of us launched into "April Springs" again.

LOST IN THE MUSIC

"*Last April the rains came down,*" sang Jesse, "*and washed away your love.*"

Dad and I joined in, harmonizing on the next lines. "*Last April the rains came down, and washed away my pride. When I lost your heart in that rainstorm, I think I nearly died.*"

Jesse pushed her microphone away and looked over her shoulder at me.

"Tennyson, your vocals need to blend more," she hissed.

Jesse always uses my full name when she bosses me around. Usually I like having a unique name, but the way Jesse says it always makes my temper rise into my throat.

"I'm doing my best," I said to her.

I like singing harmony, but when I'm singing low notes, my voice loses some of its smoothness and gets a grainy edge. Mom says that's what makes my voice unique. When you're singing backup, though, you're not supposed to sound unique; you're supposed to sound *invisible.*

"It's boiling in here," Jesse said curtly. "I need a break." Without waiting for my dad's reaction,

she stepped off the edge of the stage and slipped
out the front door.

Dad frowned. "I'll go turn up the AC," he
said, heading to the storeroom at the back of the
shop where we rehearse.

I sighed. We never seemed to be able to get
through an entire rehearsal without Jesse getting
upset—and this time it was my fault.

Mason slung an arm around my shoulders.
"Don't let Jesse get to you," he said. "She's not
happy unless she's complaining about something.
I thought you sounded great. Didn't she, Waylon?"

Waylon, our golden retriever, perked up. He's
named after one of Dad's favorite singers, the "out-
law" Waylon Jennings, and he definitely lived up
to the name when he was a puppy. He always used
to break the rules, like escaping from the backyard
and chewing up our shoes.

"Maybe the Tri-Stars should try playing some
of your songs," Mason suggested, nudging me with
his drumstick. "Remember that one you wrote
about Waylon? *Oh, Waylon. Wayyy-lon! He's a real
sweet pooch . . .* " he crooned.

LOST IN THE MUSIC

I sang the next line. *"Long as you make sure he's not on the loose . . ."*

"Wayyy-lon," we harmonized. Waylon howled along.

I laughed. "I don't think those lyrics are ready for an audience yet."

"C'mon, it's a good song!" Mason said.

"It's just okay," I said.

I'm twelve now, but I've been writing songs since I was ten. "Waylon's Song" was the first one I ever shared with my family. I was really proud of it back then. Now, though, the words seemed sort of cheesy.

"I've gotten better since I wrote that one," I said.

"Yeah?" Mason said. "You should play me something."

I hesitated. I'd been working on a few songs lately, but none of them were quite ready for any-one's ears but mine.

"I need to finish some lyrics first," I said.

"Suit yourself. Want to help me catch up on inventory while we wait for Jesse?"

We always hold Tri-Star rehearsals at my dad's

music shop, Grant's Music and Collectibles. My parents have owned the store since I was little, so for me, it's the next best thing to home. Mason and I don't officially work there, but we all help out when we can.

I followed Mason into the storeroom. It's packed with shipping boxes and instruments that need repairing. Dad was at his desk, writing *Trash* on a piece of paper that he had taped to a sagging black amplifier.

"Wow!" Mason said. "Is that a Skyrocket 3000?"

Dad nodded. "A guy dropped it off for recycling yesterday. Apparently it's broken."

"No *way*," said Mason.

"You want it?" Dad asked.

Mason nodded eagerly, his eyes so wide that you'd think he'd just won a free car. My brother loves rewiring musical gear. Our garage is full of half-fixed amplifiers and soundboards that he's determined to repair.

"Great, we'll bring it home to the workshop after rehearsal," Dad said.

Mason craned his neck to peek out the window.

LOST IN THE MUSIC

"I'm not sure we're getting back to rehearsal any time soon," he said. "Jesse's still on the phone."

I groaned.

Dad gave my shoulder a little squeeze. "Tenney, I know you're excited to practice, but Jesse's got a lot of solo shows coming up and she's a little stressed out. So let's just give her another few minutes here."

I knew Jesse was busy, but it was hard to be patient. I'd been looking forward to band rehearsal all week. If I could, I'd play music every waking minute.

"Fine," I said after a moment. "I'll go work on some of my own songs."

"Good idea," Dad said, ruffling my hair.

I ducked out of the storeroom and returned to the small stage at the front of the store. Dad lets customers use the stage to test out microphones, amplifiers, and instruments, and it doubles as the Tri-Stars' rehearsal space. I slung my guitar over my shoulder and adjusted Jesse's microphone to my height, looking out at the empty store. Waylon was curled up by the vintage cash register, watching me. For a moment, I imagined myself on a real stage, in front of thousands of people, about to perform a song I'd written.

"This next one goes out to Waylon," I said into the microphone.

I picked out the chords of the tune I'd been working on. Melody comes easy to me, but it takes me a long time to find the right lyrics to match. I hadn't figured out words to this song yet, so I just hummed the melody while I played. As the song's energy rose and washed over me, I filled the empty room with music.

The song ended and I opened my eyes. Waylon was asleep, which made me laugh. Jesse was still on the phone outside. Everything looked the same, but somehow I felt stronger inside. Playing music always made me feel like that. But performing my *own* songs for people, letting them feel what I felt through the music—*that* was my biggest dream.

Jesse came through the door and tucked her cell phone into her pocket. "Okay," she said. "Go get your dad and brother, and let's get this rehearsal over with."

I snarled and let my fingers ripple down my

guitar's six strings, sending up a wave of notes. *Jesse doesn't know how good she has it singing lead*, I thought. I hopped off the stage and headed toward the storeroom. *Maybe I should ask Dad to let me perform one of my songs with the Tri-Stars*, I thought. But I knew that he'd only agree if he thought the song was *great*. And that meant not playing it for him until I was sure it was ready.

HOT CHICKEN & BRIGHT LIGHTS

Chapter 2

*W*e wrapped up rehearsal and drove home. When we pulled up, my seven-year-old sister, Aubrey, welcomed us by doing cartwheels on the lawn in front of Mom's food truck. I love Mom's truck. It has shiny silver bumpers and it's painted robin's-egg blue. *Georgia's Genuine Tennessee Hot Chicken* is painted in scrolling tomato-red letters along the side.

Mom appeared from the open garage, her carrot-colored hair twisted up under a bandanna, and her freckly arms moving fast as she loaded food bins into the truck's tiny kitchen. She reminded me of a hummingbird: always in motion and stronger than she looks.

"Finally!" Mom said, as we hopped out of Dad's pickup truck. "We were starting to get worried about y'all. How was rehearsal?"

"Okay," I said. "But we only rehearsed three songs."

Mom raised an eyebrow. As the former lead singer of the Tri-Stars, she knew that being in a band is always full of drama. "What happened?" she asked.

"Jesse happened," said Mason.

"We sounded good, though," Dad chimed in.

Aubrey cartwheeled over to us, her sparkly tutu bouncing as she landed with a thud on the grass. "When do I get to play with the Tri-Stars?" she asked.

"Soon, baby," Dad said.

Aubrey pouted. Everyone in my family plays an instrument, but Dad is the one who decides when we're ready to perform with the band. Dad plays anything with strings. Mom sings and plays Autoharp, Mason plays mandolin and drums, and Aubrey's learning accordion. I've played guitar since I was four, and I started banjo last year. Dad always says that as members of the Grant family, we have music in our bones.

TENNEY

Mom rubbed Aubrey's shoulder. "Just keep practicing. Nobody ever won a Country Music Award by doing cartwheels onstage." She checked her watch and nodded at my guitar case. "Better get that inside, Tenney. We're wheels up in ten minutes," she said. "We need to be set up by six o'clock."

We were about to take the truck downtown to sell Mom's food at Centennial Park. Aubrey's favorite singer, Belle Starr, would be performing an outdoor concert there. I wasn't a huge fan, but I'd never turn down a chance to hear live music.

I ran into our family room with its red patchwork rug, jumble of antique furniture, and musical instruments everywhere. I set my guitar next to a couple of Dad's and raced upstairs to the bedroom I share with Aubrey. You can definitely tell whose side is whose. Aubrey's half looks like a glitter factory exploded. My side's less shimmery, and decorated with all things music. I've adorned the wall over my bed with old photos of Patsy Cline, Joan Baez, and Johnny Cash, and a framed 78 rpm record of one of my favorite songs, Elvis Presley singing "Hound Dog." My guitar pick collection

HOT CHICKEN & BRIGHT LIGHTS

sits in a glass jar on my nightstand.

As I sat down to change shoes, I saw my most prized possession: my songwriting journal. The cover was decorated with rosebuds and blooms, and I'd covered its pages with lyrics, song ideas, and doodles. With my new melody still stuck in my head, I was tempted to crack open the journal to work out some lyrics. Before I could, though, Mom honked from the driveway. I hopped up with a sigh. Writing my song would have to wait.

Request a FREE catalog at
americangirl.com/catalog

Sign up at **americangirl.com/email**
to receive the latest news and exclusive offers